*For my daughter Tlholego,
creation's finest handiwork yet.*

Planet Savage

by
Tuelo Gabonewe

The publication of this book would not have been possible without the assistance of the Jacana Literary Foundation (JLF).

The Jacana Literary Foundation is dedicated to the advancement of writing and reading in South Africa, and is supported by the Multi-Agency Grants Initiative (MAGI) through whose generous funding the JLF aims to nurture South African literature and bibliodiversity.

First published by Jacana Media (Pty) Ltd in 2011

10 Orange Street
Sunnyside
Auckland Park 2092
South Africa
+2711 628 3200
www.jacana.co.za

© Tuelo Gabonewe, 2011

ISBN 978-1-77009-751-3
Job No. 001582

Cover design by Trevor Paul: www.behance.net/trevor_paul
Cover photo by Lanel Janse van Vuuren
Set in Sabon 10.5/14 pt
Printed and bound by Ultra Litho (Pty) Limited, Johannesburg

See a complete list of Jacana titles at www.jacana.co.za

I am nine years eleven and my name is Leungo. An unlucky kid wedged with no chance of escape in a world of savages. That's me. My old man, my mom, their friends, their friends' friends, our relatives, the lot of them. There's a barbarian everywhere you look, and this is not even a creature feature.

My father is a man of medium build. He's neither sturdy nor is he slight. He's got a terrific personality and sense of humour and everything, but as far as looks go he's an indigent. I can't for the life of me imagine what it is my mom sees in the dude. Good thing my mom's genes overpowered his or I'd be in the same swamp as my old man. Here's a sketch of the fellow in question for you: he has a beard that lines his mandible in dots like an aerial view of a rural Zulu homestead. The whites of his eyes are eternally yellow, beige, like the moon at noon, and believe me when I tell you that the wise gods were feeling a great deal generous the day they blessed him with a head. You won't believe this but he's got beautiful legs, smooth and without a scar, greatly unbecoming when put together with the rest of the pieces that collectively complete the curious piece of creation that is my father. That's my old man right there. He's thirty-six five.

A knockout beauty's my mother. The prettiest face in the world, fat brown lips and all, smooth ebony skin from crown to instep, sweet white eyes, an exquisite torso with Phobos and Deimos side by side, holding up. Curves. Legs. A stretch mark here, a love handle there, but that's nothing. She's thirty-nine eleven.

We live in a township, my kind and me. We live in Tlhabane, one of the biggest, busiest locations of the North West Province. My dad works at a building materials factory or corporation or whatever the thing is called. He's been working there since the Middle Ages. Malome Jobe and company often mock him: 'I say, Rasta, when are you going on pension, bloke? Come bro, Geez, you've been working at that place forever. Take the piggy bank and run. Surely there's enough in there by now to take care of your ass until you croak?' My old man's head, the same oversized pumpkin, is smooth as a spoon yet everyone calls him Rasta. There was apparently a time in his life, probably before I was even conceived for I have sure as hell never with my eyes seen a wisp of hair on his scalp, when he wore his hair in dreadlocks. His response to the question why he doesn't take his pension and call it a day is always the same: 'That's my boy's money, boys. Anyway, you fools would kick your mother's potties if I ever left work. I'm the bishop of this clique. Y'all should start calling me Dad.'

I know immediately what he means. He says it like it's some joke but it's not funny. My dad is a thief and I'm not ashamed to say it. In the middle of the month, and this is like every month, when pockets are parched and heads are hung, it is him who takes it upon himself to drive the pack back to the river, or at least to a pond if times are really hectic. I don't know how he does it, and I've been to his place of work quite a few times and have noticed that there is always a guard on the wide-eyed watch at both the entrance and the exit of that huge hall crammed to the ceiling with building materials, but my father always escapes with *chilisi,* as he calls the stuff he plunders. Twenty-litre paints, brushes, window frames, wheelbarrows, hammers and nails, iron rods, crooked pipes that I don't know what they're called, adhesives, small stepladders, vices, the works; I've seen them all. The longest it ever takes him and the pack to score a buyer and get rid of that chilli is, on average, forty-five minutes. And so it goes: the deal is clinched and a cash payment is made, and the heaven's reservoirs' valves snap, and it rains.

We live in a square natty little house second from the corner in a fluent row of ten houses, me and my parents and, I might as well jot them in as boarders, Malome Jobe and Benedict and Ditsebe and Spirits and Selemo and the rest of the ever-injected pack. Our house beheld from outside is nothing more than a big box with dirty formerly pure white now yellowish walls and a battered old maroon slate roof. In front of the house is a gorgeous little patch of evergreen lawn, while the rest of the topsoil that is not grassed is buried under a thick layer of black gravel that makes the gums squirm when feet tread on it. The palisade in which the box that is my father's house is fenced is a work of genius. The iron rods are coated in metallic green with a touch of gold at the spear-shaped apexes; the small gate is a little archway while the large one is painted all gold and slides smoothly to the left and to the right on a horizontal iron beam. In all the decade that I have been a part of this family we have never kept a pet.

Step inside, and the box transmogrifies into a homely cavern. The house has six rooms in total. The living room, neat and kempt and beautifully furnished with leather sofas, a dark brown wooden coffee table with a little mat underneath of a colour whose name I don't know, and a television stand that carries a giant of a TV set, seventy-two centimetres or so wide, and a noisy little hi-fi that is eternally in full blare, the three bedrooms, one of which is packed with things like wheelbarrows and shovels and hosepipes and plastic chairs and used as a storeroom, a kitchen and a bathroom.

Today is one of those days. Mom is out, has been the whole afternoon, the whole day actually. She's at a hair salon getting her hair done on credit. The hi-fi is playing softly for a change. I am inside the house watching an uninteresting kids' show with the television's sound muted. A fully grown man with a beard ugly as my dad's stands behind a table carrying scissors and newspapers and adhesives and is at pains demonstrating how a whole lot of playthings can be created out of seemingly old newspapers and magazines. The pack is sitting outside, by the side of the house under a man-made canvas shade. Out of nowhere, well out of his epiglottis really, my dad's voice rises to jab the wind. 'Damn. This life. Sundays are too long and too boring when one is penniless and his beautiful wife is out punching more holes in his wallet and he's stuck with a bunch of ugly paupers three times more broke.'

The petulant quip is followed by a silence-flooded infinity. The second time around it is another voice that goes pinching the wind.

'Say, Rasta. What's the plan, landlord?'

It is Ditsebe. I know all their voices by now. They've been a part of my life for a long time. Of course Ditsebe, 'ears' in English, is not the guy's real name. He got the name from Malome Jobe, one of the two founders of the pack, when he arrived in Tlhabane and got inducted into the clan. There is of course no need for me to point out the obvious but if you're slow and don't quite get it they call the guy Ditsebe because he's got extra large funnels for ears. The dude's a man-elephant. He could swat a man to death with just one of them.

My father does not respond to Ditsebe's question, so the broke pack sits on tight, each man wrestling his brain to try to see if he will not be the one to come up with an intelligent quick rescue plan that will deliver the whole broke pack from the jaws of thirst. Somebody says something, and an argument breaks out. A blare of men's voices pervades the atmosphere and they're at it for a while. Benedict rebukes them like a headmaster when the noise eventually dies.

'What the fuck are you? A bunch of girls? Grow up. I don't know why you don't just go ahead and start a sorority. Jobe here can be the chairwoman. He's got the requirements for it, a loud mouth and an anticlockwise tiny little mind. He's probably even wearing a thong right now. I bet ...'
    'Okay guys,' my dad cuts in. 'I've got a plan. Let's get that bucket and make our own grog.'
    'Good plan, comrade,' says Malome Jobe, 'except ...'
    'What?'
    'Spirits is not here.'
    'Don't worry, man. You'll be his stand-in.'

The pack explodes with mirth. Seolo Magang, the one they call Spirits, is in terms of age the oldest member of the pack. He's in his early fifties. He's short and thick and has a round, rubbery belly under whose immense weight his belts' buckles are always bent and facing the ground as if paying some exaggerated respect to gods unbeknown. Not only is he the oldest member but he's the quietest too. He likes his drink though, make no mistake. The man drinks like a well. He's been at the receiving end of many a prank, Seolo Magang, from his comrades who draw buckets of thrills from making the oldie an object of amusement. No surprise, then, that when the clan made their first ever brew it was Seolo Magang that they called upon to be the taster, guinea pig to be more precise.

'At least you've lived longer than us, Magang,' one of the guys I can't remember who had said. 'If you should croak now you'll have led a long life still.'

'No man,' Seolo Magang had protested. 'You can't ask me to drink this thing. It looks like vomits, like human ordure all stirred up. What's in here anyway?'

'It's a cocktail, old man. Do you want me to tell you about the ingredients?'

'Please do, young fellow. Please do. I think my life depends on it.'

'Okay. Check this out, bananas are in there. Sweeteners are in there. Oh yes, a small teaspoon of yeast is in there, you know, to give the malt that creamy quality. And one and a half litres of *Skiet*. You like your *Skiet*, don't you? It's a fine brew. Come on. Down a glass for your homies.'

'Is that all?'

'Uh-huh. The lees have settled. Come on. You're the eldest. You're our father.'

And the hook caught his Adam's apple. He smiled like a child, old Seolo Magang, flattered, overwhelmed by the occasion. He opened the gates of his throat and buried a jug. It was not a brew for small boys, certainly none for elders, and you knew it at once the way the elder winced like a sissy slaughtering a cock. Of course they hadn't told him but there was methylated spirits in the mix, lots of methylated spirits. And it wasn't one small teaspoon but five spoons of yeast, accompanied by one spoonful of tartaric acid. They fed him the malt and resolved behind his back to wait for an hour or so to observe how his system would react. They did not even have to wait that long and Seolo Magang the guinea pig had hit the floor. He wallowed and bounced up and down in the viscid lake that was his vomits like a buoy. The naughty pack sprang to hover above him in a circle and Benedict went about dishing out some frantic first aid. It took forever for the man to come to, but he popped out of it eventually, dizzy as death.

Malome Jobe went in the house after my dad's suggestion for a grog to be concocted, and when he came back out he bore an empty twenty-litre bucket that once upon a time contained paint, white paint that my dad had mixed with a powder and stirred until it turned golden and smeared it sweetly on the walls inside the house. They had clearly not learned a thing from Seolo Magang's thin escape.

'Don't you boys worry about it; I'll brew the brine myself. Who knows what horrors you unmarried buggers get up to at night? Let's see. This is all we could raise. Forty-four rands and seventy cents. Come, Selemo, you're the youngest. I'm sending you to the bottle store. Get us seven hundred and fifty millilitres of *Tough Drizzle* and ...'

'*Rough.*'

'Heh?'

'*Rough Drizzle*, not *Tough Drizzle*.'

'Tough, rough, blue, green: where do you see the bloody difference, boy? Here. One *Rough Drizzle*. It'll be twenty-six rands fifty for that one. Get us ten loose draws with the change, and a sachet of tartaric. If there's still change after that you can go get your future mother-in-law a see-through petticoat. Get moving.'

'Yuck. I hate comedy when it's maladroit old men dishing it out.'

'On your way.'

My people originate from a village whose name I can't now remember, a village somewhere between Vryburg and Delareyville. It was there where the old man started school. For most of his childhood he was a lone cruiser, at least that's the story as I've heard it in dribs and pieces. It was only when he got to middle school that all that changed. A new family moved into the village, a couple of parents, a daughter and a son. The son in question, who was the same age as my father at the time, checked into Setlatla Seitiri Middle School and became classmates with my old man. Love was instant in sprouting between the blokes. A friendship ensued, the commencement of a long, crazy relationship. My dad's and Malome Jobe's eyes flare up when they remember those years.

'Remember how scared you were on the first day, JB? Heh? You looked like a *thokolosi* with that hairstyle of yours that made you look like you had been trapped in a burning kraal and you carried that rucksack on your nape like a man on a mission to a planet not yet discovered and you walked with a stoop and with your neck stuck out like an eland's. Remember?'

'I wasn't nervous.'

'You were, man. *Yessus* your zippers were wet with piss. You should say thanks I rescued you when I did. The monkeys of that village were out to shred your foreskin.'

'Get out of here. Who says *you* were tough? Don't be charming man, you brought me no security. You became my bro and they kicked us around both.'

'Don't remind me. If only I could get my hands on that Sebata monkey today.'

'Don't even think about it. Last I heard the man was old as a stone. They say he's only got two teeth these days, incisors *nogal*, hanging on for dear life in his mouth. Sad.'

'Sad? Fuck him six times. That shit gave me crap throughout my days at school. You know what, may he accidentally bite himself on the scrotum with the surviving couple.'

'I'll get drunk to that.'

And my dad carried on, gaining even more spirit as he continued to recall times past.

'And the girls were something else, boy.'

The pack sprang back to life with a collective start. Even the ever-tired, ever-bored Seolo Magang the guinea pig squirmed, slowly like a ghost stabbed in the buttock with a hot needle.

'Say, who told you all that stuff about Sebata? Is there somebody from home that lives around here?'

'No man. I went to a funeral in Barkly West a few weeks back and bumped into an old schoolmate. Some dude with a round rump and a face that hasn't changed one bit. I can't remember what his name is now. He told me and I forgot again. You know, one of those nondescript guys, like old Spirits here.'

Spirits frowned. Selemo chipped in.

'Come on, man. Your brother-in-law was about to broach an interesting topic. Forget the round-rumped bugger.'

'What interesting topic?' my dad asked.

'Girls, old man. Cherries.'

'Oh yes. Tell them, JB, how I spent long hours teaching you how to pounce on cherries.'

'You taught me nothing, man, stop lying. Everything I know and excel at I taught myself.'

'Oh yeah?'

'Ja. I taught myself everything I know.'

'And Thulagano?'

'What about her?'

'What ab... what about her? *Ek sê*, have you forgotten how she became your accessory?'

'Okay, alright. You had a little hand at my clinching her, you know. I admit. But she was the only one. In any case I'm the one that injected all that poetic poison into her skull. I administered that enema all by myself. You facilitated the meeting, sure, but that's all you did.'

'Okay, time out, boys,' said Seolo Magang with unusual, unbecoming zest. 'What's this hide-and-seek? Give us the whole story from beginning to end.'

'Right,' said my dad. 'Okay, here goes. I was tight with this girl, Ruang. Fine chick, the finest of our time. She and I were fire together. All the buggers of that village envied me, this one included. I was the man. They all wished they had my balls. I owned all of them and I loved it. This one's the only one I ever worried about since he was my only buddy and was firing blanks everywhere he trained his Adam's apple. I tried a few times to get him sorted, I did. He always flunked, until my Ruang came up with a master plan that we set up a friend of hers with my homie. I sold the bugger on the idea and spent four afternoons teaching him what to say and how to say it, and how to hold his nerve and stuff. That was one gig I didn't want him to flunk. Ruang was doing the same on the other side, selling this simian to that chick. So the week got to Friday and it was time. My chick and I made it happen. We had a scheme all worked out and we saw it through. When she came to meet me after school on Friday she came dragging along her friend Thulagano. This one nearly crapped his socks when he saw them come around the corner.'

And my old man paused for a second, groped for the bottle, stroked the red label of the *Rough Drizzle* before he took a swig.

'Carry on, man,' demanded Benedict. 'What happened?'
'The girls reached us. There was not a lot more Ruang could do so she forked off the footpath to join me and this guy in the meadows. Thulagano kept walking. She didn't even look at us, but it was more than encouraging that she had deigned to make an appearance. This one had more pain in the womb than a woman giving birth. I turned to him and said "It's time, do it. There she is. She's all yours. Come on." I knew he wouldn't move himself so I prompted him. I had to. That girl Thulagano was about to turn the corner and disappear.'
'I bet the monkey hit the road barefoot and fled,' one of the blokes said with a voice choked with laughter.
'He didn't. He took her on.'

11

'He did?'

'He did, but with some rickety pluck. He sneaked in on her like a thief. The girl stopped and let him get on with it bang in the middle of the footpath, under the screwing sun. He kept looking back at me. And I was right there, quietly spurring him on.'

And on and on went the story. The long narration eventually got to the part I knew all too well where my old man met my mom. Malome Jobe hadn't been to school this one time and my dad, for the first time, went looking for Malome Jobe at his place when bam! he stumbled on his sister. She had just come back from school. Her hair was tousled. She had eyes to see beyond the distances, legs to illuminate an ancient cave. Her skin was brown and fresh and smooth as a new calendar. Ruang's place was dismantled, taken over. Sempheng Dichoene, now Lerumo, my mother Sese as we very fondly call her. A ravishing young sylph at the time was my mother. She was a young woman then, but still older than my dad and Malome Jobe. My father's heart sprang beyond the boundaries of age and he fell in love with Sempheng Dichoene right there and then. He courted her, resolutely like she was some task that he had to conquer to win his soul the prize of immortality. She kept telling him off, giving him attitude. He kept coming. He was not losing that one. She made him graft for months, and when he was finally on the point of giving up she let the latch turn and let him in. She finished standard ten when my old man was in standard seven. He dropped out of school and they trekked together to Rustenburg. Teenagers at the time, they stuck together like lungs. Survival was not easy. They did odd jobs here and there and looked after one another. My mom found a job at a café in town owned by a Portuguese guy, a South African fellow of Portuguese extraction. He continued to do odd jobs. Together they rented a one-roomed shack in Tlhabane. They grafted for some six years not entirely content being tenants in a shaman's yard and one-roomer in the land of platinum until they acquired an RDP house, the same RDP house that is now our home. They were very happy when it eventually happened and they landed a place of their own. It was not that they had qualms with being a shaman's tenants as it was that they hated the fact that they had no dwelling they could call their own and the years were screaming past the hems of their clothes. Malome Jobe left the village and came and lived with my folks. My dad was still doing piece jobs and Malome Jobe joined him. Mom found a clerical job at the Post Office. A few months later my dad also found a proper job at that building materials place. Malome Jobe's lot was last to change. He found a job at the mines, and when he was convinced he could stand on his own two feet he found a place of his own and moved out. My father's probing arrows found my mother's pistil and my seed ruptured. Four years later and they got married. Malome Jobe agreed that he'd go with them and sign as witness, on condition he'd get something liquid and peppery for his troubles, and a striped shirt with short sleeves and two pockets on the breast. They had no choice.

My parents work hard and take their jobs seriously, and this is the one fact that sets them apart from their peers. And they are a good couple too, better than most couples I know. I just wish they'd renovate their lifestyles a great deal. For one thing I wish they'd go a little easy on drinking, and on having people haunt our home. I feel that if they can improve on these two levels then dignity might just decide to come back and hover above our abode again. Surely that's not too much to wish for.

I am still in primary school. I go to LD Matshego Primary. My bosom pal is one Legofi Dikutlo. The dude and I go to the same school. We live two blocks apart, my homeboy and I. We walk together to and from school everyday. Unlike me, my friend Legofi is not an only child. He's got a younger sister; a fair-skinned, petulant but cute little thing they call Masosi. Ntate Pagiel Dikutlo, Legofi's father, is a middle-aged man and a former colleague of Malome Jobe. These days he's got a few businesses and he's quit the mine. He's not the most social person on earth Mr Dikutlo, and not many people in the township are particularly fond of him. Some reckon he's an upstart, but I know him better than most and I think not he's a proud fellow. From what little of him I've had the opportunity to observe and study I think he's too much of a nice man. And he's got dignity too, trucks of dignity. Legofi tells me he puts a few rands aside, his father, in an account at the bank to send him to university when he finishes school, and I think that's just too intelligent. I don't mean to talk badly about my old man or anything but I've never heard anything like that coming out of his mouth. I guess there's a whole distance separating the grounds on which the minds of the two old men in my and Legofi's lives operate. Legofi's mom is a little younger than my mother, but in the arena of looks my mom squashes her hands down. She's also a nice person Mrs Dikutlo, and she's pretty much as driven as her husband. Their house is many leagues more gorgeous than ours. Expensive, well-kept furniture. Huge wall units. Nice family pictures on the walls. Tiles on the floor. Double-door fridge. Four bedrooms each with a double bed nicely made with clean linen. I guess what I am trying to say is that the Dikutlos are a nice people that are financially well off and live in a nice house. I am particularly fond of Mr Dikutlo, simply because the man commands respect. Not only that but he himself holds me in some serious awe too, you know. When he reprimands his son for not hitting the deck hard enough where his studies are concerned he tells him he wishes he could be like me. There are times when I feel he comes down a little too hard on the poor chap and that it's unfair that he should sing my praises at the expense of his son's self-worth, but I dig the respect anyway.

Legofi and I are both in grade four and we're classmates this year for the second year running, but we've been buddies for longer. Indeed my friend is a bit of a slowcoach. He is a friend of mine and I hate the way it feels like I'm gossiping about him, because I'm not. Of all the children in our class it's always him who takes the longest to understand stuff. Other children are always out to ridicule him, but I give him my support since he's my friend. He's my brother and I always make an effort to give him a hand where I can. Sometimes we get together after school and do homework together. He asks me. His father pushes him. I like the way his old man works hard to keep the boy on the points of his toes. I like his strictness. I dig his involvement in his kid's growth and education. Sometimes I wish my father would be like him. I wish he'd be a little more involved in my life. But then again poor Dad didn't make it to standard ten like Mr Dikutlo, who by the way is now attending computer classes in town every Thursday and Friday after work. All my dad knows is patting me on the back and fondling my scalp, and calling me Prof. Then his eyes descend to the sums in my exercise book, which are without a doubt a great many light years more complicated than they were in his day, and they water like he was peeling some wild onion. That's when he puts a few coins on my desk and staggers off back to his pals.

But at least the poor old stallion ever makes an effort. My mother's another one altogether. Despite the fact that she's more educated than my dad she's more ignorant when it comes to my education. I bet she does not even know for sure what grade I'm in. She used to attend parents' meetings at my school back in the day but does nothing of the sort these days. 'I'm too young to kill myself by way of long soporific drags of senseless meetings,' she says every time I give her a letter inviting parents or guardians to the next meeting. 'I can use my time better,' she once said, and I asked my dad to go the next time and he told me straight to my disbelieving face that parents' meetings are for women. I'm telling you man, these people are crazy.

Time moves fast and things change too quickly in this Tlhabane of short trees, brown grounds, short buildings and nude skies. Today there's a new guy in town; a new, curious creation of a man. He is, by the look of things, the new owner of the empty house a few yards away on the opposite side of the street. The previous owners were still around two days ago, if I'm not mistaken. I did notice yesterday though that the curtains were not there, and I've not seen them since. I used to like the old man of that house. Old Ntate Sengwegape. Nice Madala. One of the few men in our zone who were never slaves to alcohol. To be honest I didn't know the man all that well until he came bursting into our yard one time and treated me and onlookers to a hilarious spectacle. I think it was two years ago. It was just after sunset. I was lying on a mattress on the lawn thinking about going inside to go chill in my room when the gate flew wide and admitted a man who I initially thought was Spirits as I saw him pasted against the darkening sky but who got closer and turned out to be old Sengwegape. He did not greet. His throat was hot as a cinder. He opened his mouth and set the cool evening on flames.

'Rasta!' he cried. 'Rasta.' His voice was hard as a sack of stones when it hit the ears of those within hearing distance. 'Rasta. Please tell me, man. Tell me it isn't true. Tell me you're not coming onto my wife.'

The pack rose to a collective level of attentiveness I'd never seen. My father shifted, swallowed, started to answer. His voice was full of cracks and quavers and I knew at once that the pawprints in the chicken coop belonged to his hoofs.

'What are you talking about, old man? Me and your wife? Your wife and me? What are you saying?'

'You know exactly what I'm talking about. You saw her out on the street last night. You accosted her. You touched her where only I am allowed to touch her. You asked her for things. Dammit, Rasta. What is wrong with you?'

'Get out of here, Sengwegape, man. You're crazy. Where did you hear all this crap?'

'Weren't you talking to my wife last night?'

'Well ...'

'Well?'

'I don't know, man. I don't remember. I don't know. I guess I may have seen her out and greeted her. But touched her? Gee, old man. Touched her where?'

'You scoundrel. You monkey. *Bliksem* man, your wife has just about the roundest, freshest, brownest backside in the whole North West Province, and you go and finger my wife? What's with the greed, man? Huh? Why is your heart so full of sticky serum like that other thing? Come on, man, leave it.'

And he was off, spitting rapid things that only he could hear and understand as he trundled his old man's shapeless body off into the massive throat of intensifying dusk.

'He's mad,' said my dad after the elder had made his exit. And the pack buried its black milk in stunned silence for a period until Malome Jobe could not hold himself anymore. He broke out with a spear-sharp laugh and kept at it until the thin hours. He absolutely loved that kind of thing.

The new guy in town is just that, a new guy. It appears for now that he has moved in alone. And he's an odd design alright. He walks up and down the street all day, to and from the shop buying things one by one, possibly an attempt on his part to get himself used to his new environment. Fish oil. Maize meal. Tinned fish. Light bulbs. Mosquito coils. He's at it the whole day. Curtains shake non-stop as his movements up and down continue. Tiny children, barefooted and barebreasted, follow him up and down. They walk in a group. They wait until he's almost at his gate and they double their pace. When they're close enough to do so they go together at once, in unison like they've been practising the chorus since they were very small.

'*Agee.*'

He greets them back, only I can't hear what he says. And they run to the corner full of amazed excitement where they wait for the man to come out again. I hear them as they pass by my house, whispering with childish disbelief.

'Did you hear? He speaks Setswana.'

They stand standby guard at the corner for about an hour and he doesn't come out again. Dejected, they walk away.

Spring has come and gone and now we're getting ever so close to the commencement of our final school exams for this calendar year. Because his father is not great on the idea of us being alone at his house in the afternoons me and my friend Legofi, lest we start getting naughty and break stuff, Legofi spends almost all his afternoons at my place. When we come back from school we stop for a while by his place. He goes inside to change into normal clothes and I wait for him under the tree outside in front of his parents' bedroom's window. He re-emerges with two bread rolls split symmetrically and smeared with fishpaste, hands one to me and we amble out to my place. My folks are still at work when we get to my pad. I open the door and the windows and put on the box and go to my room to change. When I come out of my room I take out the ice cubes tray and we chill out a little in the lounge, feasting on ice. Then we take to my room where we spread all sorts of books and equipment over the rug by the side of the bed and wallow in sums for hours at a time.

Another day at work has been conquered and taxis crawl in and out like ants and spit people off at different points. A rare thing happens today. Mom and Dad come home together. He may be a hundred metres out but my father's hunger for the black milk is as clear on his face as the sun is on the sky. If anyone deigns to give them any attention it is only because he is with Mom. They come in. Mom does not waste time but plunges straight into the labour of cooking. The old belle cleans the house before she leaves for work every morning. My dad goes to the main bedroom to lie on his back and stare at the ceiling and the gate makes a sound admitting tonight's first arrival. My dad never tires from entertaining his lousy friends.

It's evening. It hasn't darkened up yet, and people passing by the street can still be made out clearly. My dad and Benedict, Benedict who has probably the greatest appetite for the drink and is seldom absent, sit outside with their heads hanging low as if they were a sad duo recently divorced by their wives and now being put on display behind a transparent glass in the middle of a busy shopping centre on month-end and not finding it one jot pleasant. They are not talking to one another, just sitting together. Neither are they drinking. There's nothing about their feet. A figure emerges, a familiar-looking figure. My father jumps so high he almost hits a dent on the ceiling of the sky. It is the youngest member of the pack; the handsome, lanky Selemo on whom rumour has it Benedict's wife has or used to have a cock of a crush. Now my dad speaks.

'*Bliksem,* man, *kante* how long does it take for the taxi to get here from town? Heh? What the fuck took you so long?'

'Sorry, bro Rasta. It was JB. He made us bounce from one bottle store to another, comparing prices.'

'Where's he now? Where's our liquor?'

'He'll be here just now. He's down the street with some pink guy that he says he knows from work and he's got the fluids.'

'Some pink guy? What pink guy?'

'Some guy, bro Rasta. I've never seen him before. Oh, here comes JB.'

Malome Jobe comes prancing in, and he's got a plastic bag in his right hand and the left one is deep in the pocket of his flowing pair of formal trousers. In spite of everything he dresses quite nicely. As a matter of fact he is the best-dressed guy in this whole pack.

'Don't even greet us, you fag. Give us our stuff and go skinny-dip in the toilets at the taxi rank.'

'Ha-ha-ha funny, extremely funny. You've got no right to complain, bud. I'm not your child. I'm nobody's child.'

My dad and Benedict lunge forward at the same time. Malome Jobe springs, and they miss him. They get on his tail. He runs circles around the house and they chase after him. Five rounds later and they haven't gained a centimetre on him. They stop chasing the tittering cockerel. They're not amused. They're actually irritated, like seriously pissed.

'Hey, Selemo,' says Benedict out of breath. 'Run with your young knees and catch this bugger, will you?'

'Not a chance, old-timer. I've been on my feet all day. The only things I can move after all today's battering are my eyelids.'

'Fine. You can start peeing in your glass this minute. You're not getting a teaspoon of that malt.'

'Jobe, come on, man. Grow up,' says my father starting to get doubly annoyed.

'Apologise,' says Malome Jobe.

'For what?'

'I don't know. Just apologise, man.'

'Cut out this crap. Come on. You're starting to get in my bloomers right now.'

'You amuse me, brother-in-law. You remind me of the grandmother I never had.'

Malome Jobe puts the bag down and the hungry couple

tears into it like jackals. They go through the first round rapidly and dead quiet, until Malome Jobe breaks the silence.

'Hey guys, I think there is a possibility our family is going to grow by another member. There's a new guy in this street. Dimpaletse. I used to work with him at number eight but now he's at the new shaft in Marikana, the one that opened last year. He's the new guy that's moved into our friend Sengwegape's old house. As a matter of fact I think I should go fetch him this minute and get him inducted. Get the constitution ready. I'll be right back.'

Malome Jobe makes an exit and returns a few minutes later with the new guy in tow, the same one who's been marching up and down the street all day.

'So he's the pink guy you were talking about, hey Selemo? My goodness, boy, you were right. The man is pink as a dummy,' says Benedict as the men approach.

'Here he is, boys,' says my uncle Jobe. 'Meet Dimpaletse Prince. I'm sure we can call him Dimpa, or Dimpampa. Dimps, welcome to my family man.'

'He banna,' Benedict exclaims. 'What kind of name is Dimpa? And what species of human being are you, new guy? Are you a white man gone bankrupt or what?'

The pack explodes with laughter. He doesn't know how to respond to that one, the new member. He mumbles something that only he can hear. Indeed he is of a puzzling ilk. His hair is long and woolly, his nose is long and is not shaped like our noses, and he is extremely fair-skinned for somebody that goes by the name of Dimpaletse. I wait for him to speak out loud. He does, and his Setswana is as spotless as that of any other member of the pack. But his accent is different. Benedict picks that fact up and his eyes well up with excitement. The ice with which he received the guy melts.

'Where are you from, Dimpa,' he asks the man.

'Warrenton. Kgomo-ka-Beke.'

'*Bliksem*, that's far,' says Benedict again and plunges into another one of those crazy laughs of his where his throat seems to become one thing with his large intestines and his shoulders rise and fall like he was a puppet being electrocuted.

'Aren't you at least going to offer me a seat, fellows, and perhaps a bite at your water?'

'Don't you have a backside man?' asks Malome Jobe.

'I do. That's why ...'

'Sit on it.'

'Come on, man.'

'Fine. This is the first and the last time I'm going to go get you a chair. Watch where I go, alright, because you're on your own next time.'

He goes around the house to the back and there gets two chairs from the set of eight that the pack has bought especially for their get-togethers that are in all honesty an everyday thing. Malome Jobe throws one chair at the new guy and sits on the other. The man catches his chair and sits. The pack goes on getting on with it and nobody offers the new guy a sip. He is very talkative, this new guy. He is definitely one that can talk the hindlegs off a black mamba. My father's quiet as a cockroach. I don't think he likes the new addition to the family very much, and frankly I myself am struggling to find in me an iota of fondness for the man. His voice is dry as dust, his accent very funny.

23

He tells horrible jokes and laughs at them himself, with a throat filled with pebbles, and red blood sprints from all corners of his body to converge on his wrinkled temples. He's very unpretty, and his mannerisms are kind of very unrefined.

The hours are getting smaller and the liquid thinner, and the poor chatty long-haired fair-skinned new guy has not been offered one sip. A few more bites by the members of the pack and the liquid is extinguished. Benedict, as always, is the first one on his feet. He looks for it and finds his shirt on the lawn. He puts it on, and is ready to take his leave. He says goodbye in true barbarian style: '*Fotshek*. I'm getting out of here.' Selemo and Ditsebe get on their feet and follow Benedict on the way out, each armed with an unopened bottle. When Malome Jobe stands up to leave the new man roars.

'You guys. *Yessus*. You guys are terrible.'

Malome Jobe smiles, turns to my dad.

'Say, Rastaman. What's your neighbour on about?'
    'You're asking me? Isn't he your friend? I'm going inside boys. Sweet dreams.'

Malome Jobe takes the chairs back to their place behind the house and returns to tell Dimpaletse Prince that it's time to go.

'Rule number one,' I hear him tell the guy, 'When men drink you drink. You don't wait for an offer; you don't wait for the green light because chances are you'll see none. What are you, a chick? Come, let's get our backsides out of here. Come on, man, let's go. You sober monkey. You're sober, aren't you? Aah. Don't you just love the smell of my breath? Don't be so sore, man. What are you, a pimple?'

The next day he waits, Dimpaletse Prince, for the pack to get together and get going again. He's got revenge on his mind. They come together. Ditsebe, Selemo, Benedict, and Malome Jobe – they all make it in time. That's when he makes a swaggering entrance with a six-pack of yellow bottles that I have never seen before. He grabs a chair and sits at a distance from the others. My father will have none of it, especially since he doesn't like this brother one bit.

'You're making a mistake, Pinky. In my kraal you drink with all the bulls or you don't drink at all.'

Sadness tumbles on the man like an electric blanket cast down carelessly by the sky in a fit of anger. He brings his chair closer to the bunch, and his heart has hardly hammered a hundred times and his six-pack is no more. These guys don't mess around.

'*Bliksem,*' cries he, and I know at once that he's now a full member of the pack.

Exams are over; the festive season is almost upon us. My friend Legofi and I watch TV like all the sets on earth are about to be repossessed and destroyed. Some days we wander around the township and bump into our schoolmates and hang out with them. I envy my friend Legofi. His parents have promised him a camera phone if he should pass with satisfactory grades this year. My case is guaranteed. I'm going to get the best grades in the whole school, but my parents have promised me nought.

I don't like to say this but it's true: all my folks care about is splashing a lot of dough on their own entertainment. I wish they'd actually go out of their way every now and then to remember that they've got a child that needs a bit of personal attention.

We're in the last week of November. Tonight Malome Jobe arrives with a bag. He tells my old people that he's staying over, that he's had a fight with his wife. He says it's nothing big and my folks shouldn't worry.

'But we've got no space, JB. We don't have an empty room. Where are you going to sleep?' asks my dad.

'I can sleep with Prof. I don't mind.'

'I don't like it. I don't like the idea of you drunk and disturbing the peace of my boy. The only place available will be the living room, and that means you'll be getting up very early. My son's bedroom is off-limits.'

'Come on, Masimong,' says my mother intervening for the fellow that took the nipple immediately after she quit it. 'I'm sure the child won't mind.'

'I don't know. I don't like this. It's a single bed Leungo has in there. How the hell are they going to fit in a single bed together?'

'Come on now. You know the bed is big enough. We slept in it together before we bought our queen, remember?'

'Fine. But you must go back tomorrow and sort things out with your wife. My boy needs his space.'

For a change Malome Jobe is quiet and does not brush what my father says aside as a lot of blue baloney. When they're done negotiating he comes to my room.

'*Heita* Prof. I'll be sleeping with you tonight. Don't worry.

It's only for tonight, perhaps tomorrow night as well. Then I'll be on my way. How's that? I promise I won't snore.'

'No problem, Malome. Don't worry about it,' I say. But I know I'm lying. I hate nothing more than people coming into my space and asking to share it.

So the sleeping arrangements have been sorted. Malome Jobe goes to the shops and returns with a bottle of brandy, red meat wrapped in a brown paper and two litres of orange juice. The juice is for me and the brandy for the grown-ups. For a change the members of the pack, Benedict included, have stayed away tonight. It's only my uncle and my folks tonight, in the house and cosy. Mom takes the meat to the kitchen and browns it adroitly. The two grown men and I sit in the living room and watch a football match on the box. The guys aren't swearing a great deal tonight, their team is doing well. They are all smiles and clean words. My mom feeds us. I eat my food quickly and disappear to bed before she gets an idea to make me wash the dishes.

It's late in the night, I don't know what time. I hear footsteps, my bedroom door opening, and murmurs. It's my dad and Malome Jobe. I pretend to be fast asleep.

'Look at him,' whispers Malome Jobe. 'The poor *bliksem* thinks he's a foetus.'

They giggle like mice, leave my room and into the bathroom. I stalk them in the dark with a ninja's delicate steps. They stop at the toilet, open their zippers and pull out their water pistols.

'*He monna*,' cries Malome Jobe pulling his leg out of the way. 'You're peeing on my shoe.'

'Sorry, man. That's because your shoe smells like the

toilet. Fuck, it's a mighty horn you have JB, heh? Who'd have guessed, skinny bugger like you?'

'That's me, my dear boy. No one in this town comes close to me. You included. Y'all are a bunch of teenage boys.'

'Get out of here. This thing's a fucking dud. Tell me, has it ever peed a child, huh? Exactly.'

'You're just jealous.'

'Jealous? Screw you. You're impotent.'

'Impotent? Me? You're talking crap, man. You're lucky the chick you're with is my sister, or I'd show you who's impotent.'

They're almost done. They wag off the last drips at the same time and I sneak back to bed.

We're in the first week of December. The festive season is here, people stay up forever and go to bed very late. Dimpaletse Prince, the new guy, is a new guy no longer. The kids have outgrown their fascination with him. They don't find him interesting anymore. They don't greet him when they pass him on the street. They've got a new fascination the children of my neighbourhood. Dimpaletse Prince's household is swarming with fair-skinned, cute young children. There's about five of them in total. The twins whose names I've heard, Tshidi and Mosidi. They look like they could be three to four years older than me. They wear identical camouflage pants with pockets on the sides. They're growing breasts, small oval things each a distance away from the other. I don't find them very attractive. Then there's the youngest child who must be three, the second youngest who must be six or seven. There's also a baby that for reasons known to myself I'll leave out of this. And then there's the finest of them all who must be the same age as me. Gorgeous is nothing, that chick is blazing hot. I saw her today still, and almost peed myself admiring her beauty. She wore her hair in three ponytails, each bound in a pink ribbon. Her clothes were as bright as were her legs, and she brightened up my mood. One of these days I will ask my dad and the comrades to let me have a swig at their milk, and once I have acquired a lot of pluck from the liquid's quick currents I will go look for her and sing in her ears like a swallow. The man's wife is in town too, and she's brighter than the man and all the children combined. Mom says she doesn't like her but I think she's okay. She could be my future mom-in-law for all I know.

The festive season is getting older. The guys drink like they are scheduled to have their bellies surgically removed in January. My mother's drinking has also increased a notch. My dad does not always like it, Mom drinking with him and the men. They sometimes get out of control when they are stoned and start messing with Mom by making perverted comments or getting too close, physically, for my dad's appreciation. The norm is for my dad to pinch one bottle and sneak it in the house for Mom to enjoy while she cooks and relaxes after a long day at the Post Office. That is how she's got by for most of the year. But now my aunt is here, my aunt Sebeto, Malome Jobe's wife. Not quite as precious as Mom but pretty enough. They arrived here last week, she and Malome Jobe, with bags and suitcases containing things that are apparently all their possessions on this earth. They maintained their rented room was broken into just before they trekked out. They said the break-in had led to a major argument between themselves and the landlord and that had led to their receiving marching orders. My dad thought it was all a lot of bull. They went into a small caucus, the four grown-ups, last week when the other two reported and got me sent out to the shops so I wouldn't sit in and listen. When I returned from the shops my dad was smoking, sulking, nestled in a corner as if hiding from the world. My mom told me Malome Jobe and my aunt Sebeto would be staying with us for the rest of December. She said they had been unfortunate and lost their old room and that their belongings were stolen. But when there was no one within earshot my dad cornered me and told me the truth. Malome Jobe had been caught stealing at work and had been fired on the spot. His rent payments were also three months outstanding and the landlord had decided to hold on to his furniture until he got what was due to him.

'Don't be like your uncle when you grow up, Prof. Don't be like me. Be a better man than all of us.'

'Don't worry, Dad,' I said to him, and we went back inside.

Malome Jobe and my aunt Sebeto have 'borrowed' my bed, so on a nightly basis I pull out a slender mattress from behind the wardrobe in my old people's room and unroll it over the rug next to my bed in my bedroom. I pull the rug a considerable distance away from the bed that is for the time being my uncle and his wife's bed.

Today is only the third day since my uncle and his wife moved in with us but my mom has already drawn up a cooking roster. All Sundays she has given to my aunt, and for every week until New Year's Eve she's got three days and the other woman four. I was there when she revealed the roster to my aunt, and she did not complain.

I'm trying really hard to be a pleasant cohabitant, but this is really a hard time for me. I don't like it very much when there are people in my immediate personal space. It ticks me off in a huge way. I've never been used to it. It would be a great deal better if I could at least be alone during the day, but I'm not. Aunt Sebeto is not employed and she stays with me the whole day through, everyday. She gets in my way and she gets on my nerves. I try not to be a pustule and complain to my mother. Aunty comes into the living room everyday at one o' clock when the nicest cartoons are on and asks to watch the repeat of, wait for it, the soapie that she watched without blinking the night before. I don't like to be rude so I let her have her way. I endure. I sit with her and watch grown men kiss other grown men's women and wait for half-past. Malome Jobe's back to piece jobs until he finds something stable again, one day, whenever that will be.

The evenings are noisy, way noisy. My dad and Malome Jobe never run out of it. They don't work at the same place – my uncle has nowhere to call his place of work since he's always all over the place – but they always arrive together. And the same old thing happens. The women cook up and dish up and supper is scoffed. Then grown-ups make merry and I slither unnoticed to bed.

I'm something of a heavy sleeper. Often I don't hear Malome Jobe and his wife when they come in to sleep, but I do hear them once in a while. They undress not in the dark but in the naked brilliance of the light that they put on when they come in. I sleep with my blankets pulled over my head. They take their time, then they climb the bed and the old springs creak and groan non-stop as they roll about and adjust their bodies over the hollowed but comfortable old mattress. I don't hear what happens afterwards because ghosts of sleep kidnap me just in time. In the mornings, starting at half-past four, my mom and dad and Malome Jobe get up and take turns using the bathroom. My mother is usually the first one in and takes forever to come out. The blokes only need about fifteen minutes between the two of them. We wake up at round about nine o'clock me and my aunt Sebeto. She cleans the house and I wash the cups and bowls that the early birds use before they leave for work. The real dishes are washed every night before bed by the woman whose turn it is in the kitchen according to the roster. We eat breakfast when we're done with our chores, and then we sit in and bore one another all day through.

Beginning of December's week number three and everybody is on leave but Malome Jobe, Dimpaletse Prince and my dad. Malome Jobe is frustrated. He frets. He threatens to punch his employer full on the neck so his Adam's apple capsizes and he doesn't enjoy his Christmas meal because he's mean and making it impossible for him to enjoy *his* festive days. My dad draws maximum amusement out of Malome Jobe's frustration. It is only a few days now until Christmas Day. My mom and Aunty Sebeto are at pains tonight putting together a list of the things they're going to buy tomorrow. We go to bed early tonight me and my mother and Aunty Sebeto. The two old boys join their cherished others outside and predictably enter another marathon.

The next morning I'm shaken out of slumber by my mother's hands. I am dreaming. I am in a fist fight with my friend Legofi. Legofi is huge; he's a giant. He's actually smaller than me at the beginning of the duel. I give him a hammering. But with every blow he swells and grows taller and butcher. At last my punches can't seem to shake him at all. I feel like I'm punching a tall dummy made wholly out of dead rubber, or an awkward, gangling slab of flab. He stalls around, gets himself used to his new size. The he brings it. The last blow I see before I pass out is an uppercut. It catches me on the chin and lifts me off the yellow-and-blue rug (we're in my bedroom). I am suspended in the air for a moment, and then I return to earth and hit the floor with all front parts of my person at once. My skull cracks into two and I clasp my hands around my head to prevent my brains from spilling on the floor. There's blood everywhere. I am splashing about in my mess, quivering like a croc caught in the snout by a steel trap. A force shakes me violently. I open my eyes, not in a hurry, to see at last what it looks like on the side of the dead. I see a familiar face pasted against a white endlessness. It is my mother. The white endlessness at length turns out to be the white ceiling in my bedroom.

'Wake up, child. Your aunt's going to bath in here quickly. We must leave at six if we're to make it there and back in time.'

My mom and my aunt are going vegetable shopping in Magaliesburg. I never understand the crazy things grown-ups sometimes do. I mean, there are more greengrocers than traffic lights in Rustenburg, and the two ladies have decided they're going to trek miles in search of veggies? They say they expect to be back by eleven, at which time they will go and buy groceries in Rustenburg.

'Go sleep on the couch in the sitting room so long. You'll come back when your aunt's done. I'm going to use the bathroom.'

'No need,' says my aunt. 'The child can just jump on the bed and pull blankets over his head like he always sleeps and I can go on and have my bath. He won't find peace in the living room with those two up and about.'

'Okay. Come son. Quick. Jump on the bed.'

I find the bed with my eyes closed, jump into the warm blankets that are still redolent of my uncle and his babe and bury my head in them. Aunty Sebeto rolls my mattress with the blanket and pulls the bundle to one corner. Then she leaves the room to go get her bathing water. I hear her and Mom in noisy activity in the bathroom where she draws her hot water. Then something hits me like Legofi's last blow in that stupid dream, a helluva monkey's brainwave it is. I'm not a naughty kid, really I'm not, but mightily attractive is this idea that pierces my heart like a quill and that I can't pull out. My mom and dad are drinkers and have a lot of lousy friends and everything, but they've raised me well. For what it's worth, they have raised me as well as any couple of parents can raise a child. But I tell you now this thing that's poking my head is mighty. It kicks conscience sharp in the groins and sends it flying off out of my system and shuts it out. I can't turn back now; I don't think I even want to. So I go ahead with it. I manipulate the blankets until I have a clear but discreet birdwatching opening, and I wait. I'm at the door of death with excitement. Exciting times these.

Aunty Sebeto comes shuffling back into my room. She bears a plastic bathtub in her arms half-filled with steaming water. She goes down to set the tub down on the rug. I take a long draw at the musty air inside the covers. I am tense as a witch on her first night on the job. It comes. She puts her hands crosswise around her body. She clenches. She lifts. The light nightie obliges. It peels off her skin in a graceful upward cascade. For the first time in my life a fully grown woman who actually plucks my buttons stands half-naked before my trespassing eyes that are red with excitement. It is only a lacy small piece of deft needlework keeping the prickly pear out of visual reach, otherwise everything else is out to be devoured with eyes.

She kneels beside the hip bath on the yellow-and-blue rug. She dips her washing swab in the water, takes it out and rubs a skinny bar of green soap against it. The swab absorbs a deal of froth. She scours her face, her neck, descends to the torso. She caresses her belly with the frothing cloth, bends over and scrubs her back. Then she dunks the cloth in the water again and takes it out again and rubs the emaciated ghost of a bar of soap against it. She puts the swab on the chunky brown talismans. Slowly, she starts rubbing the cloth over them. She's facing straight in the direction of my peeping corridor. She puts the cloth under one globe, the left one, jerks up the mamma and scratches the area underneath it. She pulls out her hand and the monster settles back in its cradle and I want to cough. She does the same with the other monstress. Then she dunks the swab in the water and rinses it and dries her face and torso.

She gets on her feet. It's time, surely it is. I hope Malome Jobe will find it in his heart to forgive me one day. If I should die in the next fifteen minutes I'll be the happiest corpse in all the morgues of this planet put together. She puts her fingers between hip and garment on either side, and she starts to force the thing down. The item puts up some resistance and I want to jump over and give her a hand. I'm restless. I'm sweating. The garment succumbs eventually. It hits the floor in a soundless bundle and she steps out of it. My heart moves into my throat and gets stuck. Now when it throbs tears ooze out of my skull, tears of animal joy. I love my aunt, I do. The prickly pear is in my face, and I am dead. Nothing can beat me out of this rigor mortis. I can't feel my legs; I can't feel my blood's corpuscles swimming in my veins. It is only the brown assegai I can feel. I think it wants to tear its pouch to ribbons and escape and go to war. She steps into the hip bath, bends to dredge the swab up from the basement and in an up-and-down movement sinks the swab in and out the water and wets her legs that I realise for the first time are quite fair. She holds the green phantom against the cloth and rubs it over her one thigh. She moves to the other leg quickly, and she's getting closer and closer all the time. At last she hits the CBD. At this stage I'm a dead man breathing. I'm back in the boxing ring, not with my friend Legofi but with an animal, an alligator with two legs. The fight is the shortest ever. The thing strikes me full on the skull with a heavy tail and I die. Next I'm in a black zone and I'm not even groping. I hear the sound of water as harshly as though it were the rumble of thunder, but I can't see no more.

I come out of it a period later and my aunt Sebeto has finished washing. A lacy thing similar to that other one, only one of a different colour this time, cleaves snugly about her hips and neighbouring parts of her body. The two brown charms bobble up and down like two gorgeous heads in some nodding marathon. With a series of delicate rubs she anoints her body with a nice-smelling lotion, combs her short hair and covers herself up in a tight-fitting sleeveless blue dress that is v-shaped at the breastbone and has an inner waistband thing that makes it hold her waist tightly and is of a silky, stretchy material. What a woman. I'm even afraid to clear my throat for fear the covers will go up in flames and pin me against the springs of this bed and fry me alive. My aunt searches for something in a box behind my bed, digs out a pair of pink sandals and puts them on. She lifts the plastic bathtub filled with soiled water off the floor and exits the bedroom. The sandals make a clicking noise that a few days ago irritated the crap out of me but that I don't find irritating anymore. She's in the bathroom. Her and my mother's voices fill the house up to the roof beams. Mom is slow, I know her. She isn't finished yet using the big marble bath in the bathroom. I've seen Mom naked too, a hundred times, and not once have I ever been moved like what just happened now. She's got a mighty scar just above her waist, my mother, but she is still too pretty and my dad and I love her to bits. Aunty Sebeto pours her soiled water in the toilet, flushes it. The old thing spews a gush and hisses like a dinosaur when its cistern refills.

It has been some two hours since the grown-ups took off. The two women went to Magaliesburg, Malome Jobe to his part-time job. My dad was supposed to be off today but his employers asked him to come in because there's an overload at work or something. The last one to depart, my dad, called me out to lock the front door when he made away. The ladies were already at the gate and Malome Jobe was nowhere where I could pick him out. I said see you later to my dad, locked the door and scuttled over to the window. If the windowpane did not know how to absorb secrets without wincing it would have burst to powder with shock as steaming air filled with mad things left my nostrils in chunks and lammed against it. She walked between my mom and dad, my aunt Sebeto Dichoene, and even beyond the windowpane and the green-and-gold palisade she was as ravishing as a deity. I returned to my bedroom and found that the aroma of her lotion and green soap amalgamated wouldn't let the great grip of its claws on the air let up. I jumped back into bed and a long empty stretch of time elapsed.

I am awake now. The clock in the living room announces with an amount of annoyance to my enquiring eyes that it is thirty-four minutes past eight. For a change I leave the TV alone and put on the radio. A jock with a high-pitched, irritating voice is at pains trying to link up with a traffic reporter and failing to reach him. 'This guy Greg deserves a fine for turning without indicating,' he says out loud. He laughs like a creature at his own flop of a joke. I can't take anymore of it. I turn the dial. I stumble on a station that I don't know and probably don't like but anything is quite welcome that will offer me instant liberation from that rasping bugger. The first song is bad on the unknown station, the second one even worse. An instrument of music that I can't tell if it's a trumpet or a saxophone whistles out aloud, and dies, then a needle-sharp voice breaks out of a woman who sounds like a poor-sighted madman is breaking a small pimple on her bum with a pair of pliers. A live record, or a song recorded live. People scream, and shush. The instrument goes again, only a little softer this time. Then a little applause that dies quietly. I've had enough radio for one day. I switch the thing off and put on the TV, and what do you know, nothing interesting on the box either. I go into the kitchen and concoct a little meal for myself, and wolf it all in a couple of bites. From there I go to the bathroom and clean up. Suspended on invisible clews for time is a slouch that is always idle, only getting by because it moves on false wings, as Benedict once said when he was feeling down in the pit toilet after a long session at it, another ostrich of a December day's away and in flight.

The gate makes a noise. I look out the window. It's my dad. He's the first one back. He's got a huge checked bag that looks like the ones house-to-house vendors like to use to carry their merchandise. He finds me in the living room. Thirteen hundred and twelve hours on the point is the time.

'*Heita* Prof. Are they back yet?'

'No. Not yet, timer. You're the first one back.'

'Heh? *He banna.* So where's your girlfriend? Did you tell her to hide quickly under the bed when you saw me come in?'

I know he's only teasing me so I don't reply. He goes to his and Mom's bedroom and there dumps the bag. He puts on a black cap with a straight white peak.

'Listen, Prof, I need to run to the shops quickly, and then there's this guy I need to go check up on here in GG Section. If your mother should get back while I'm still out tell her I'm in the neighbourhood stretching my legs. I'll be back just now.'

He gives me a note to buy myself whatever I want and takes off.

It has been some forty minutes since my dad landed and took off again when my mom and my aunt arrive. A van driven by a man whose oval face I've never seen stops outside the gate. The van's canopy is flung open and a whole garden is transported into my mother's kitchen. The driver that is a hundred things but handsome receives his pay with a grateful swoop and takes a kick at the pedals. The old lunch box refuses to do anything for a while, then it flies off like a rocket. One can only thank

39

the ancient gods, seeing the performance of this battered piece of work right now, that the girls made it back and safely.

Mom and Aunty are done packing away the stuff in the kitchen. They come into the living room, kick off their sandals and throw themselves on the sofas.

'Go to the kitchen and pour us some cooldrink will you, son?'

I take my time before I do what my mother asks me. My aunt Sebeto is on her back on a long sofa, her legs hanging. Her head is only a few centimetres away from my hand that lies on the arm of the one-sitter that I am sitting on. I want to extend my arm and stroke her scalp and tell her it's alright, that she'll be feeling better in a minute. The floral dress clings on to her body like it were one thing with her skin. I know what lies beneath. What a feeling. I want my future wife to be just like her, brown and smooth and fit as a kudu. I can't feel my breath; I can't feel my heart beating. I stand up and go to the kitchen to carry out my mother's bidding before something in me goes off.

The fridge is packed with vegetables. There's a number of healthy-looking fruits too. There's only one bottle of cooldrink in the mix, two litres of red liquid in the holder of the door of the fridge. I take it out. I turn the cap and the bottle belches like a prophet. With two glasses full to the brim and vomiting in my arms I walk like a chameleon out the kitchen back into the living room. I return to the kitchen for my own glass and back to the living room to join my beloved girls. They lounge with me for just a brief time, just until enough energy has returned to their bones.

Then from nowhere my mother speaks a cue, and they get on their heels again.

They are gone for three-odd hours, and my dad's still not returned when they get back. There can be no escaping this one. It has to be me. I pull the wheelbarrow out of its sleep in the storeroom and trundle it at the speed of that other man's van to the corner of the street where a minute ago the taxi dumped my mother and my aunt and a Tlhabaneful of groceries. I fill the barrow up with only a quarter of the stuff and push it back to the house. Mom follows me with a few bags and my aunt stays behind to keep an eye on the rest of the stuff. We've come a long way in Tlhabane, we really have; but there are still a few scoundrels that refuse to move forward with the rest of us. Some people opine that those *bliksems* if they knew where the keys were kept to the control room of the sun they'd steal them and break in and tamper with the wires until the whole system was so messed up there'd never be daylight again. Just the other day, and on a Sunday morning to boot, we were called out of our bedrooms by a whistle's cry after there had been a break-in at the corner house. The man of the house was hysterical as an untamed horse. His voice was full of venom as he shared what happened with the small crowd that had gathered quickly as soon as the whistle had sounded.

'They stole everything,' the man told the curious crowd comprised of this boy and a few young fellows and my dad and his bunch and a whole population of women dressed in transparent nighties through whose pores, black nipples and round areolas, that looked on each woman like twin birthmarks, could be made out. The women wore towels around their waists and had many interpretations of what the man told them as they further relayed the story to late arrivals. 'DVDs, DVD player, TV, computer, plates, mats, curtains,' the man had told us. 'They cleaned us out. They even stole my wife's panties.' At that announcement Malome Jobe lost his shell and burst out laughing. 'I didn't know his wife had any panties,' he had said. My dad did not see the funny side of any of it. He was not hanging around. 'I'm getting out of here,' he said. 'Computer? Computer my knee joints. What does this one know about computers?'

The mob followed my dad's lead, and the man and his family were left alone apparently waiting for the police.

Today my mom wakes up early, and wakes me up. We wash together in the bathroom, she in the marble bath and I in the plastic tub, the same one my favourite aunt washed in the other day. I hurry her through breakfast and we get moving. I'm excited. There is a big buzz already when we get to my school, as there is a buzz at Bosa-bo-Sele Primary next door. We enter the big yard. My mom goes to my classroom that I point out to her and where my teacher is busy handing out reports to parents. I join a bunch of chaps that aren't really my boys while I wait for my mother to get my report and come back out. She comes out eventually and there's neither a smile nor a frown on her face.

'Let's go. Come.'
    'But I want to see my report.'
    'Forget it. You know what's likely to happen if I give you this report now while we're still here.'

She pouts her lips and adds fuel to her steps. She's talking from experience. Last year this time I took my report from her and went through my results with a fine comb. The teacher had given me eighty for Setswana. I lost it. I searched the place and found my teacher, confronted her. I stood there fuming and made her mark my script again, and when she was finished I was up in the nineties. 'Happy?' she asked me. I said yes and apologised and Mom apologised and we stepped. This time I have to trot a few blocks after my mother before I can have a look at my report card. The road seems unusually long and it's a long time later when we reach home.

'Okay. We're home now. Can I have my report please?'

I open the report and what I've always known is confirmed. I killed it, again. It's straight As all the way. I'm elated. I hand the report over to my dad. He opens it, has a look, and his eyes wet up.

'Where have they written Passed, son?'
    'No, Dad. They don't write Passed anywhere. Not anymore. They write Achieved or Achieved Beyond for every passed subject. Look, I got Achieved Beyond for all my subjects. I'm a genius.'
    'That's my boy. I've never told you this, Prof, but you take after me.'

He pushes two blue notes into my back pocket, a sloppy job really, because Mom catches him in the act.

'*Bathong*, Masimong. How can you give the child so much money? Leungo, give me back those notes.'
    'No ways, Mom. It's mine. Papa gave it to me. It's mine to spoil myself because I'm a genius.'

'Oh really? You want to go and spoil yourself, huh? And what are you going to eat in January back at school?'

'*Ao Ma*. Don't tell me you weren't watching the news last night.'

'You know I wasn't. What ...?'

'The weatherman was a clever one. He says it's going to rain baked eggs and fresh loaves all month next month.'

'You think you're a funny, Leungo? I hope your sense of humour will still be with you come January next year.'

'Come, Sese. Leave Prof be. It's only a small gift you know,' says my dad.

'A small gift? Huh? Small, Masimong?'

And she leaves the living room in something of a huff. My dad pats me on the back, smiles. Mom is just being unnecessarily unreasonable.

The afternoon is fiery today. People arrive early from work. My dad is already in another planet when Benedict, Selemo and Ditsebe arrive. Spirits comes through, then Dimpaletse Prince and his wife soon thereafter. The two women that are permanent residents in my home are in the house, so the bright woman goes in to join them. It is evident from the way they bury the malt that the boys are in a race to gain on my dad who's been at it the whole afternoon. Not a very long time passes and Malome Jobe is in the house. He's not alone. There's somebody with him, a familiar figure. It is the old lost-and-found part-time member of the pack. My favourite guy is back, this guy who is so funny it hurts. His name is Maitirelo Malehonyane but we all call him Mighty. Great dude. I love him madly. I almost jump to my feet and run to the gate to give him a hug.

'Hallo, hobos,' says he, greeting his comrades that he has

not seen in a long time. '*Yessus*, I should have known. You're still wearing the same clothes as last Christmas. You haven't taken a bath once, have you? You rascals. Queue up and kiss my knees, boys. I'm back.'

'Sit down and stop making noise, you fool. You'll make us sober with your ranting. Say, JB, which grave did you have to dig to find this old remain?'

'Still a funnyman, Rasta the landlord, I see. You know what, for that silly effort at a joke all the drinks you and your grandchildren will ever consume and puke are on me.'

The men sit in a circle and drink their bellies into balloons and ridicule one another and laugh with throats that get drier by the sip. Malome Jobe's the loudest bugger on earth, period. When he laughs his lungs seem to bob up and down and sideways in his ribs like that small ball does in a whistle when blown. He particularly enjoys it when there's somebody being ridiculed. All the members are present today, and there's a whole racket in the air. Ditsebe tries to call Benedict by name and gets it wrong like he always does when he's filled up. Benedict goes mad. He throws his body forth in Ditsebe's direction. He lifts him by the shirt front and brings their faces close together until they're almost kissing.

'I'm not Bennett, you idiot. I'm Be-ne-di-kt. You're still a fucking teenager, man. How do you bloody get such a simple name messed up? Heh? This is the shit that comes with young men who hang out with seniors. Your head works like shit these days. We should never have taken your backside in.'

'Take your hands off me old man. I told you to stop watching wrestling, warned you this would happen. You've become a little bully all over again. And I'm not your child, man. Stop insulting me.'

Malome Jobe laughs; he never lets the opportunity to have a chuckle go for nothing. My dad is annoyed.

'Kill one another, boys, and help us prove to those that never knew before that no one attends funerals on days like these. We can do with a fewer lips on the tap anyway.'

They separate, take their seats again. The madness continues. They have grown tired of ridiculing one another so they take it to the vendors that go up and down the street on foot and on bicycles.

'How much?' Mighty calls out loud when the ice-cream man's bicycle goes by. The man puts on the brakes. Old rascals burst out laughing.

'Is somebody calling me?' asks the ice-cream man.

'Are you crazy? Can't you see we're consuming grown men's drinks?'

'F'k,' exclaims the man out loud and kicks the old machine into movement. My father whistles, waves. The man draws a U on the road and returns to my father's palisade. My dad calls me over and gives me coins to buy myself ice cream. I take the coins and go out the gate and dig into the big box and retrieve a lemon-flavoured parcel, pay for it, and the man rides off less angry the second time around. Less than five minutes elapse and the second victim comes marching by, with a stoop and a serious-looking face that make him an even more ideal object of drink-driven mockery. They whistle. He opens the gate and enters. Poor vendor. He's got a bag so big and so full it's hard to imagine how he managed to get it zipped up.

'Howzit?'

He nods his head. Malome Jobe's already laughing.

'What's in the bag?'
    'Clothes,' answers he. 'Clothes for small children and women. Nice clothes.'
    'Oh yeah? Let's see.'

He unzips the bag and one by one they haul the stuff out it. They put the stuff on a chair and in the man's arms and they keep digging until they reach the bottom. They can now almost touch the ground. Malome Jobe's face flares up, and I know at once that there's something out of this world down there. His hand comes out slowly, and there's something in it. It's a thong, a beautiful small thing that compels the men into a moment of silence like it were a totem unearthed by mistake when the royal, the elderly and the long-departed had passed word that it was not to be handled by a mortal for a hundred eternities. Malome Jobe holds the thing in his fingers for a moment, loving it, and then slowly puts it back in the bag.

'Sorry, man,' he says to the vendor. 'We don't have money. Christmas spending has punched holes in our wallets. For real. Maybe next time.'

The man puts the rest of the scattered stuff back in the bag, evidently pissed. He holds the bag between his knees and zips it up and sets off without saying goodbye. No doubt about it, that lacy red thing still has the comrades dumbstruck.

A few minutes later two young guys open the gate and

come into our yard. Young nicely dressed guys in their early twenties or so. One carries a clipboard, the other a file. They greet the stoned men who greet them back with grunts save for Selemo who says out loud: 'Hello, clean boys. Isn't it a bit too early to be wearing Christmas clothes?' Nobody laughs.

The spruce fellows introduce themselves. They say they have been sent by the municipality to go around the township handing out warnings to those whose water and lights accounts are in arrears to pay up or else.

'Or else what?' asks my dad sitting up a notch on his chair like a jock on top of a speeding filly.

'Or else your water supply will be cut off, sir.'

'Listen here, boys, alright? You go back to whoever sent you here and tell him that I dare him to come himself, so I can make him clean my toilet with his underpants. I don't have time for none of this crap. Tell the municipality I don't take kindly to shitty threats. Now get out of here before I hack your baby penises off your waists. Move. Get out.'

The guys hasten to put a typewritten page on the ground and put a pebble on it to keep it from being blown off by the breeze, write something on the clipboard hurriedly, and leave. The young men have barely made an exit from the gate when another guest comes through. A young boy that goes to Motladi Kgwadikgwadi Primary and that I've seen many times before but that I don't know by name. Son of the man the pack calls Kgatampi. Kgatampi is of course not the boy's father's real name. His father knows my dad so he came to hang out with the guys one rare evening. He introduced himself to the group as Gabriel but got a new

name before he'd been there for an hour. It was Benedict
who gave him the name. Kgatampi he called the man, after
Kgatampi the madman in an old African folktale. There
was, once upon a time according to folklore, a young man
in a huge village who stood shoulders above his peers in
many spheres of life and who was adored by men and
women and young children alike. All the fathers in the
village turned down offers of *magadi* for their daughters.
Until they received offers of *magadi* from Kgatampi's
uncles they made sure their daughters remained fine
virgins, unmarried and available. The witches got jealous;
according to the story the witches were vengeful mothers
of rebuffed young men. They bewitched him. They sent
a bee to sting him on the nape, right on the point where
the spine meets the brain. The bee's sting was wicked. His
head swelled bigger than a watermelon. He lost it. He went
mad. He developed an instant hatred for young women.
He chased after those who passed by his father's compound
daily to flaunt tantalising small breasts whose nipples
perched deliciously high up on their udders, teasing the
skies. He whipped them hard. He drew weals on their bare
backs with a sjambok. The king heard about his madness
and sent men to take him prisoner and return with him
to the royal kraal. He beat the king's men up too. One
morning he stormed out of the village and never returned.
He fought wild animals without weaponry and killed them.
He uprooted trees just for the madness of it, and in the
process turned the forests, and literally so, upside down.
One day he came one on one with an elephant. He armed
himself with a stick and attacked the beast. He rushed in
on the beast, hit it on the knee with the stick, so hard that
the stick broke into splinters. The beast went wild with
fury. It hit him square on the head with its heavy snout. He
ran into the wilderness with blood pouring out of his nose,

mouth and ears and died in transit. Wild animals ate him, and their blood froze in their veins and they died.

'Malome Rasta,' says the boy in a man's voice. 'My father said I should call you to one side and ask you for something.'

My father stands up and steps with the boy to one side. The boy says something to my father that I cannot hear. My dad goes into the house, comes out, returns to the boy and hands him something. The boy clasps, utters silent goodbyes and springs off.

'Hey, Rasta. Isn't that Kgatampi's boy?' asks Benedict after the boy leaves and my dad joins the pack again.
    'It's him. It's Gabriel's boy.'
    '*He banna*. You and that Gabriel.'

He senses he's about to be made fun of so my dad puts on a serious face.

'Me and Gabriel what?'
    'You and that Kgatampi. I smell an alley cat. There's something you're not telling us. *Ek sê*, you're not brothers are you?'

Benedict's face lights up. He thinks he's on top of something. He cries out loud: 'That's it. You're brothers. I've pieced it up. I should have caught it earlier. You both have pumpkins for heads. Why, you're brothers. *He banna*, you are siblings. Kgatampi's a relation of yours. Unbelievable.'

My dad fumes like a brand new steam pot on the stove full to the lid with smelly tripe.

'Don't be crazy, Benedict. Don't fucking be mad, man. Don't be a twat now. Please.'

'I'm just playing, man. Don't swear. I'm only kidding. You've got a pumpkin for a head alright, but nothing like Kgatampi's pumpkin. Thinking about that guy's head I'm glad I'm neither a barber nor a milliner. Drink, Rastaman. Don't be angry like a woman. You know I'm right when I say that you and Kgatampi have huge heads. It's not an insult. It's the freaking truth. *Yessus*, if you fellows paid a visit to a hair salon on opening day there'd be no staff there to service the customers the next day. They'd all be bedridden with fatigue. Sometimes I ask myself if your dreams even play out in real time like ours.'

He stops, belches. He grabs a bottle and swigs.

Almost thirty minutes pass and my father doesn't take one bite at the malt. At last he gets on his feet fuming and tears himself away from the bunch. He's pissed off. It's written all over his movements. He continues to hold a beer in his hand without downing it. He dodders off and goes and stands in the far corner of the yard, sulking like a child. He trains his eyes on the ground and keeps them fixed on one place. He takes two more steps forward, turns his back to the street and leans on the palisade. At last his belly can't take the punishment anymore. The acids threaten to eat up the intestines. The intestines threaten to coil themselves around the spine like a constrictor and suck his brain out of his skull. His hand rises. His lips find the bottle's nipple. He suckles, suckles, stops and sulks again.

Benedict tears himself away from the bunch to go and check up on my dad.

'Don't drink alone, man, or you'll go mad. What kind of host are you anyway, leaving your guests to their own devices to come stand in the corner like a scarecrow that has come to take its job a little too seriously? Huh?'

'Leave me alone, Benedict. You've insulted me enough for one night. Go back to your friends and crack some more jokes.'

'Come on, man. You're our homie. You can tell me what's eating you up and we can solve it quickly and take our backsides back to the well before those buggers forget about us and go all out. What's up?'

'You want to know what's up? So you didn't hear yourself insulting me, eh?'

'Not that crap again, man. Grow up. Don't be like a little girl. You ...'

'You want to hear something, Benedict? Next time you call me Gabriel's sibling there'll be repercussions.'

'What are you gonna do?'

'I'll tear your skin off your ass and sew it back on inside out.'

'You're talking nonsense, Rasta. You know your way back to the stream. This caucus is over.'

Benedict takes off cussing and goes back to join the others. My father mulls over something for a minute, and follows him.

Night is falling. I'm about to go in the house to do I can't remember what when Dimpaletse Prince's wife almost collides with me in the doorway. She puts her index and middle fingers in her bra and retrieves a cellphone that trembles hysterically and flashes a bright blue. She checks the screen before she takes it up to the ear to answer the call.

'Hello. Please hold,' says she to the wire. Then to me: 'Please give the phone to Lesego's father. It's a call for him.'

I take the cellphone from the woman and it's hot as a stone. The sooner I get it off my hands the better. I hold it with index and thumb like its a dead man's handkerchief and I rush towards the pack and hand the thing over to Dimpaletse Prince. He steps away from the bunch and speaks on the device for nothing more than five minutes. When he's done he gives me the cellphone to give it back to his wife, and he goes back to take his seat among the men.

I'm about to go into the house again when for the second time I almost bump into Lesego's mother. This time the cellphone has already been drawn from her bra and is held against her temple. She's on the phone for ten, fifteen, twenty minutes. Dimpaletse Prince can't take it anymore. He gets on his feet and scuttles across to her, seizes the phone.

'Bye bye,' he says into the phone before he presses the red button and terminates the connection. Then he turns to his wife, keeping his voice low.

'Who was it?'
    'Who?'
    'Don't mess with me, woman. Who's this you were on the phone with for thirty minutes?'
    'Arone. I was talking to Arone.'
    'Arone?'
    'Yes. Arone.'
    'And who the hell is Arone?'
    '*Ao Ntate.* An old schoolmate. Some guy I used to know.'

'Old schoolmate, huh? Don't be stupid, woman. You've been out of school for what, a hundred years? Do you think I'm that simple?'

He pushes her to the far corner where there's little light, and when he thinks nobody can see him he pinches her on the stomach. The defenceless woman squirms and wriggles like a millipede.

'What are you doing, dear? It's not what you think.'

She sings this chorus repeatedly and continues to wiggle as the madman pinches her belly some more. I've never seen anything like it. I want to do something to stop it. This guy has no right coming here and assaulting his wife in my father's compound. I won't let him. I move in on them. He tries to shoo me off but I don't move a toe. Let him try and touch me too.

'What are you looking at?' he asks me. I don't answer. I don't like this man. He stops pinching her. I don't walk away and he doesn't like it. 'Go home,' says he to his wife at length, and he goes back to the men.

I catch a glimpse of tears in Dimpaletse Prince's wife's eyes. She hurries back into the house. She says goodnight to my mother and my aunt Sebeto, tells them something has come up. She says goodnight to the men and makes an exit.

'*Ao banna*. Why's she leaving so early?'
    'She's full of nonsense. I told her to go to bed,' answers Dimpaletse Prince proudly.
    'Nonsense?' my dad chips in. 'What kind of a word is nonsense to be used by a man speaking of his wife, man?

What is the matter with you?'

'Nonsense, Rasta. Nonsense is nonsense and that woman is full of it. You know, sometimes I wish the sow would take her farrow and get the crap out of my life.'

'Okay, buddy. *You* can go home and go to bed now. You've talked enough shit for one month. Get out of my yard. And don't come back here tomorrow night, or the night after, or next year. I don't like you, man. I've never liked you.'

'Come now, Rastaman. Heh? Be a bro, man. Don't be like that.'

'Get out, you shit. *F'sek.*'

'*Kante*, what's your problem *monna*? Heh? I didn't swear at you *mos*.'

'You want to know what my problem is, hey Pinky? I hate idiots that disrespect their wives and ...'

'Now wait a minute, dude. I never interfere in the way you talk to your wife or treat her. You have no business telling me how I should treat mine.'

'Get out of my yard, Dimpaletse Prince, or I'll whip your pink backside blue with that hosepipe on the lawn. Just go. I don't want you here. *Fotshek.*'

'Jobe, please man. Talk to this brother-in-law of yours.'

'Huh-uh. I'm not getting involved, man. I'm just a drinker and a tenant around here. This guy's the landlord. He calls the shots. Do what he says and get your backside out of his gate and there won't be trouble.'

'You guys,' cries Dimpaletse Prince, and stumbles off.

'Sweet dreams,' calls Malome Jobe out loud after him.

We all wake up late this morning. I pull the blankets off my head to catch the fair legs of my aunt touching the floor. We go to the bathroom together and brush our teeth standing side to side. We all come together in the living room and my mother serves us tea and soft white bread.

Malome Jobe has a bottle by his feet that survived the mass murder last night. We've hardly touched our breakfast when fingers knock on the kitchen door. I go to check. It is the banned guy.

'Is your dad up?'
   'Yes.'
   'Will you call him for me, please?'
   'He's having breakfast.'
   'Please, kid. I want to talk with him.'
   'Fine. I'll go call him. Don't come inside or he'll beat you up.'

I go back to the living room. I tell my dad that Dimpaletse Prince's at the kitchen door asking to see him. He does not move an ankle, my old man Masimong Lerumo. He says he'll attend to the guy when his breakfast is finished and has settled in his stomach, otherwise he'll either puke or get indigestion. It is only some ten minutes later that my dad stands up to go have a listen at what Dimpaletse Prince has to say. He finds the man standing behind the house like a nervous shepherd come to report to his cruel master that a beloved ox has been missing for a week and cannot be found anywhere. He wears a red vest and red shorts and black morning slippers. My dad doesn't greet him.

'What do you want?'
   'I've come to apologise.'
   'What for?'
   'For stealing your roof last night just before it started to rain. Come on, man. I've come to apologise for what passed between us last night.'
   'No need to apologise, Dimpaletse Prince. Just go back to your wife and children and treat them with respect and

we might just get along better.'

'Does that mean …?'

'It doesn't. Go home.'

'What did he want?' Malome Jobe asks my dad a while later.

'He wants me to lift the ban. He's sorry about last night.'

'And?'

'And nothing. He's still banned.'

'You're tough.'

'He's a *bliksem*.'

'Come on, man. He …'

'Leave it.'

Our gate does not admit another guest until later on in the day. My friend Legofi has come out of hibernation. He's got new clothes on and walks with some newfound swagger. It's good to see my boy. I meet him at the door. It's been a while. We hang out. We lounge together in the living room and watch a DVD. My mother and Aunty Sebeto come in halfway through our picture and ask to watch a talk show, so we relocate to my bedroom. At least it's not to get busy with schoolwork this time. We play wrestling on the yellow-and-blue rug next to my bed in my bedroom. I twist Legofi's arm and pin him against the rug while I hold the hand against his back. He flails like a croc. 'Stop, man, you're hurting me,' he cries. I don't stop. He cries out loud. I let his hand go at once.

'What's wrong, dude?'

'Nothing. My back is sore, that's all.'

I don't believe him. He's hiding something.

'What is it?'
'It's nothing. Forget it.'
'Take your shirt off. I want to have a look.'
'You're not a doctor, man. Let it go.'
'Come on, man. It's me.'

He's reluctant. It takes me forever to get him to cooperate and strip his shirt. When at last he caves in and takes his shirt off my eyes are greeted by a great horror. The kid has a whole embroidery of lines that suggest a thorough flogging job was done on his back. My heart melts, throbs in my shoulders. I don't know what to say. I've never seen anything like this.

'*Bliksem*, Legofi. What happened?'

He's about to say something when my father walks in on us. He sees Legofi's back just as he's putting his shirt back on. The horror of it gets my dad. He leans against the wall. The whites of his eyes almost eat up the blacks. He comes closer to pull up his shirt and examine my friend Legofi's back.

'What happened, son? Who did this to you?'

Legofi wants to cry. He looks puzzled, doesn't seem to know what to say. He's terrified. He looks like he wants to find an opening and run.

'I must go,' he says at length. He pulls his shirt back down.
    'Don't be afraid, son. You can trust me. I just want to know who did this to you, that's all.'

Legofi hesitates. My father prompts him with his eyes.

'It's my father.'

'Your father,' cries my dad. 'Your father did this to you?'

'It was my fault. I promised him I was going to pass but I failed. My dad says I'm stupid and a money-waster. I've disappointed him.'

'He said all those things, and beat you up?'

Legofi nods. His skull is full of tears but he doesn't let a drop escape. My dad rises, shakes his head.

'Tell me son, when did your father beat you up?'

'On Monday and on Tuesday.'

'With a whip?'

Legofi hesitates. He's trying to hide something. My dad prods him again.

'Come on, son. Talk to me. What did your father beat you with?'

'He beat me with a pipe.'

'A pipe? What kind of pipe?'

'I don't know what kind of pipe it is. It's a plastic pipe.'

'That's it. You're sleeping here tonight. Let your father come looking for you.'

The pack has come together as usual and plunged into yet another drinking marathon. Legofi, in spite of his terror that has him turning to look at the gate every thirty seconds, seems amused by the pack's crazy talks and behaviour. Somebody breaks wind, a fart so foul it's almost deadly. Selemo springs to his feet, points a long accusing finger at Benedict. Benedict does not like it one bit. He snaps.

'You've no respect, Selemo, you know that? I'm old enough to be your mother's sugar daddy but you always take me for shit. Learn some manners, man. Be civilised. Learn a little respect.'

'Okay, okay. I beg your pardon, Madala. But you can't just come and break wind while we're sitting together. You could have gone to the toilet. You're the one who's disrespectful.'

'I'm warning you, Selemo. Rasta, Magang, don't just sit there and let the boy rip me to shreds. Tell him I'll fuck him up, maybe he'll hear you.'

'Okay. Okay. Time out.'

Benedict is sitting down struggling for air when a car pulls up outside our gate. It's late, and my friend Legofi has been having a tough time sitting still in the last forty minutes or so. The car's horn goes once, twice, three times. Legofi's face is purple with fear. He wants no more trouble with his dad. He gets on his feet and starts to get going, the moment my old man's been waiting for. He tears himself from the pack and comes scuttling towards us to stop the boy from making an exit. He grabs Legofi's hand and pulls him back.

'Don't go to him, kid. Let your father come in.'

Legofi starts to cry. I'm also starting to get quite nervous about this whole thing. I can't for the life of myself imagine what's going on in my father's head.

'Don't be scared, son. All is well.'

At last Mr Dikutlo loses his patience. He gets out of the car and leaves the driver's door open, comes charging into my father's compound like a bull.

'*Agee rra*,' he greets my father. His manners are dirty. He turns his attention to his kid who stands trembling between him and my dad.

'Legofi, is there something wrong with your eyes, boy? Huh? Don't you see it when it gets dark?'

'Leave the kid, my friend, take it up with me. It was my idea. The boy wanted to leave hours ago and I stopped him, told him he was going nowhere. I wanted you to come looking for him.'

'Listen here, man, I don't know you and you don't know me. You and me are not and have never been friends. Your son is friends with my son. I don't like your son much. He teaches my son stuff that I don't like my son learning that he no doubt learns from you. You had no business holding my son here against his will. That's kidnapping. Now take your drunkard's hands off my boy and let him go and there'll be no trouble.'

'The boy's going nowhere.'

'I'm warning you, man. Let him go.'

'What? You're going to beat me up? Huh? Bring it.'

'You're not worth it, man, believe me. I'm not the type that goes around getting into fist fights with nipple-wits. You've irritated me enough now, okay? Game over. Let me have my son and leave and you can go back to your friends.'

'But I told you already, the kid's staying the night. Get in the car and go home.'

'Listen here, man, you're a mere drunkard and I am not. I'm an educated man. I know people, real people. I can make this a very unpleasant Christmas for you. I can just snap my fingers and get you taken in for kidnapping. I'm asking you for the last time – let the kid go.'

'But I don't want to. What are you going to do? Call the cops. Please do. I'm sure they'll love to see your boy's back.'

Sucker punch. He did not see that one coming. He doesn't respond, not immediately. When he does at length his voice is ten times thinner on arrogance.

'He's my son. Parents discipline their children whichever way they choose.'

My dad charges into the man like a ram. He pulls him by the shirt front and I know at once that something's about to go down. He's simmering, my pops. I move in closer, so does the pack. We make a circle around them. I want my dad to hit the pig hard on the nose with his pumpkin head. I want to see the intruder's blood. I don't like this man one bit.

'You beat this boy again,' says my father, 'and goodness knows I don't care that he's your son and not mine; I swear I'll shove a hot iron rod up your intestines.'

At the conclusion of this passionate warning he pushes the man away. Dikutlo trips on something and springs back to his feet quickly. The wet lawn has smeared a green stamp on the side of his cream-white chinos. He glowers at my dad, lifts a fist into the air. My dad doesn't blink. The man brings his hand back down, seizes his son by the arm and drags him out of my father's yard. He slams the driver's door so hard the windscreen probably cracks. He steps on the pedals like that other man that came to deliver my mom and my aunt the other day and his barrow disappears into the bustling township.

The atmosphere stays sombre for a while but when enough time has passed things go back to normal. Nothing else worth mentioning happens tonight. I go inside to watch television with my mother and my aunt. They're watching a movie with the sound muted, chatting and chilling. It doesn't even look like they're watching the picture at all. The film has an age restriction of eighteen. Next to '18' are the three letters I love: NVS. My mouth slavers. Something inside my clothes turns to stone, in advance. I jump on a sofa and they don't chase me out. They're too engrossed in chat they don't even realise that I should not be in the audience for this one. I hope I've missed nothing, at least not the part represented by the letter N. That's always my favourite part in any movie. I don't wait long. A man with a narrow waist, long hair and broad shoulders parks his car outside a joint whose blipping emblazonment reads *Boobie-Trapped*. He gets out of the car, shuts the door, lights a cigarette and sits on the bonnet. The cameraman's lens sweeps over a city that's in full neon glory. The man smokes the ciggy to the stump and throws the stump to the ground. He starts moving towards the entry of *Boobie-Trapped*. He comes across a man on his way to the doorway; they bow swiftly to one another. Our slender-waisted man progresses to the entrance. He enters the building. Lights are on, and off, and on, and off. It would appear as if the music is loud and electric, but of course I can't hear a thing since the sound is muted. He walks past a group of young women. One of them puts a finger in her mouth and eyes him hungrily. He winks at her and walks on by. He gets to the tables, or stages, or pedestals, or whatever the platforms are called where the real events in joints like these take place as I've seen in one or two flicks before. He goes to the one where a curvaceous lady in a yellow bikini and a feathery scarf does it like a peacock. The woman does magical things with herself. I steal a look at the two women with me on this side of the screen and find to my relief that none has her eyes on the monitor. A senior man that sits very close to the table leans forward and very generously deposits a couple of green notes in the woman's panties. She throws her hands in the air like a nymph. She works her left curve like a belly dancer on cannabis. She leans on a shiny pole, brushes her back against it and goes down to touch the floor. She tugs the straps of her bra loose, and I remember December the 17th as the day my aunty showed me the universe without even knowing it. She rises slowly, the curvaceous chick on the TV, and goes down again. She moves closer to her audience. The senior man deposits another note. The woman rises, works some magic with deft fingers and before I can say ahem the bra hits the floor in a bundle like a shot bird. A man comes to the darker side behind the platform. Discreetly, she draws the funds out of the last garment between herself and total nudity and hands them to the guy in the dark. She returns to the pole and without further delay peels the last piece of clothing off her. The senior man's eyes glint, I'm sure mine do too. I catch a glimpse of grown-up hair. Our guy with broad shoulders and a slender waist pouts his lips at the dancer and sets out. I have seen enough. I go to my bedroom to lie on my back and cool down. I'm tired of being a child.

The next day is not as eventful as I anticipated. My dad and Malome Jobe spend the whole day alone. No other member of the pack shows up. Dimpaletse Prince skulks outside the gate and whistles a tune and my father ignores him. I don't know what to do with myself. I feel like hanging out with my guy Legofi, but after the episode last night I know that he will not come and visit me any time soon, and it is totally out of the question that I should go to his place. At last Dimpaletse Prince disappears into Tlhabane. He returns an hour later carrying a green-and-red box. He holds his nerve and comes into my father's yard for the first time in a while. He greets the two gents, grabs a chair and sits. Nervously, he lifts the open bottle and drinks. My dad does not stop him. Malome Jobe laughs out loud. All seems to be well.

Tomorrow's Christmas, and my mother and my aunt are planning to do something special for the whole family. They tell the men about their plan and the brothers dig the idea. Dimpaletse Prince rushes to his house and returns with his wife and their daughter in tow; Lesego, my favourite woman anywhere on earth. Everybody has sprung to activity. There's a sudden big buzz and a lot of movement. The afternoon's a dream. I play with Lesego, and every now and then they send us together to the shops. She speaks with an accent that's magical to hear. I carry her on my back all the way to the shops. When we return it is her turn to carry me. I wrap my knees around her ribs and my forearms around the flat area that will one day be her bosom. She tries to stand upright but she can't. I'm too heavy for her. We laugh together. No worries. I carry her again and we go back to the buzzing house. Ditsebe and Selemo arrive late in the night and they're so drunk they have to put their hands around one another's neck to stay on their feet. I wish Lesego could sleep over, but of course that's impossible. I walk her to the gate and we split.

We wake up early on Christmas Day. My dad has bought me nice garb especially for today: a short-sleeved blue shirt with buttons, a matching pair of so-called dirty jeans, and a pair of blue Slimmo takkies. Children don't wear Christmas clothes anymore, so I block off the hunger to put on my new rags. The last thing I want is to become the laughing stock. I'll see my clothes on the 31st.

Selemo reports early today, as does Benedict. The women toil in the kitchen; the men move their canvas tent from where it is and pitch it up in front of the house. Two tables are put under the shade and covered with bright lace tablecloths. The pack's chairs are scrubbed clean and put around the tables. Dimpaletse Prince helps out with more chairs from his house. I walk with him to his house to collect the chairs. I don't know why but I don't hate him all that much anymore. Let things go well, and he'll be my father-in-law yet.

The women finish cooking at around eleven-thirty. They take quick turns having a bath in the bathroom. When they are done my mom tells me to go wash up and wear clean clothes. I do so quickly. I come back outside to find that Spirits has come out of hiding. He looks troubled, but then again with Spirits one can never know for sure if what you see written on his face is the real story. He is with a chubby girl that must be twelve or thirteen, or fourteen. He stuns everybody when he smiles broadly and introduces the chick as his child.

'*Bathong*,' my mother and my aunt cry together in unison. My mother proceeds to ask him:

'*Ao*, Seolo Magang. You never told us you had children?'

Seolo Magang seems to enjoy their shock. He cannot stop beaming.

'I know. I couldn't have told you a thing about it, my dear comrade's wife, because I myself didn't know a thing about it. True. I'm telling you. I never knew I had a daughter on the face of this earth. She showed up on my doorstep only two nights ago, accompanied by a long forgotten ex-partner of mine. This little woman is such a good thing and has such great manners I have no doubt the whole thing that she's my child is true. She's got my attributes. I'm lonely, and I didn't quite realise it was this bad until they came back to me. I want to marry her mother. She tells me her mother's involved with somebody at the moment. You see, she and I didn't really get the chance to talk. She dropped this missus off and had to go. She'll be back to take her in the new year, then we'll talk. I don't buy that story about her seeing somebody. She's got a child with me. She's mine. I'll make her see reason of course. We've got a duty to help this child come of age, properly, and we can only achieve that if we raise her together in a proper family structure. She mustn't be selfish. I need her too, just like this child needs her. I can't bear this loneliness anymore. All I do is work and get drunk and go to sleep. I need a lot more.'

Everybody laughs, everybody but Seolo Magang and his new daughter who's busy giving me the eye and making me uncomfortable. I wish she'd stop it already. She's not my type. I'm more than happy with Lesego Prince.

My mom and Aunty Sebeto and Dimpaletse Prince's wife are almost ready to serve lunch. My good mood's beginning to wilt out of shape when Lesego comes strutting in, bright as a flower. And she's right on time, my love. She comes in and takes a seat next to me. What ecstasy.

The food is served, and it is yummier than anything we've had all year. Brown meat, white meat, salads, beetroot, fries, porridge, curried rice, baked potatoes, sweet peas, macaroni, the works. There's enough chow to feed a whole squad of rebels. Spirits and his daughter sit side by side and eat like hippos. The kid does look like the old man, now that I'm paying attention. We continue to lunch in silence; even Malome Jobe is keeping quiet. I wish we weren't in the company of grown-ups, then I'd do the romantic thing and feed Lesego, or I'd put my hand on her legs and run my fingers through their fawn down. These boys don't play. The last bone is chewed and the plates are removed and taken back to the kitchen. Ten minutes later and the women emerge again, with dessert this time. Lesego's eyes light up. Apparently she loves dessert. The whole pudding thing is a chick thing, sure, but if this one loves it then I love it too. Two bowls of custard and jelly, a bowl of plain sundae, triangular slices of chocolate cake, and a fruit salad – peach and apple slices soaked in strawberry yoghurt, sprinkled with black raisins. After dessert, dessert that all the men but Seolo Magang say no thanks to since it does not go down particularly well with their kind of drink, everybody gets on their feet. The males take their chairs back, and their canvas shelter. The tables are folded and taken back to the storeroom. Lesego and I sit on the stoep under the sun that is not very hot since there's a bit of cloud cover building up. There's chemistry between this chick and I, lots of chemistry. We get on like twins, like puppies. I tear myself away from her for a minute and go to my room to return with a box full of playthings. She takes a look in, dips in her hand. She decides on a jigsaw puzzle first up, and her wish is my obedience. She spreads the chopped-up cardboard pieces of a picture on the stoep, gets busy reconstructing the piece under my very keen eye. How I wish it was the pieces of my heart she was putting back together, leaving her delicate fingerprints everywhere on my pump. She is at it for a long time, and I don't hurry her. We've got all day. I'd watch her all year if I had to. She gets it right at last, and it's a picture of two birds flying into a blue infinity, their wings outstretched.

'I love it. I love this picture.'
　'I know. I love it too.'
　'Really?'
　'Yes. I love it very much.'

Now that she's done with the jigsaw puzzle she dunks her hand in the crate to look for something else. Her hand comes out with a pack of playing cards. She asks me to play a game with her and I turn her down. I don't know why but I hate cards personally. I'm surprised this pack is still in the chest. The chubby girl has been watching us from a distance, pining for a chance to join in. Now she sees an opportunity, and seizes it. She shuffles in on us. 'I'll play with you,' she says to Lesego. I don't think Lesego digs the idea of playing cards with this one. She pouts her lips and looks turned off. I leave them to it, go in the house for a pee and a glass of water. I have not been gone for five minutes but there's already a war going on when I come back out. I come out to find the chubby girl pinning Lesego to the stoep, spanking her. I lose it.

'Get your fat hands off her. Let her loose, you hear me?'
　'Make me.'

She's a bully. What the … I don't know what to do. But surely I can't just stand here and do nothing.

'I said get your hands off her. What, are you deaf? I'll kick you in your privates. I'll kick you till my shoe disappears.'

I'm out of control. I'm hysterical. I never use offensive

language. I have not emitted a swear word once all year, but look at me now. There's a whole fleet of them coming out of my mouth like a disease. Lesego's crying. I promise Spirit's ugly daughter a beating like none she's ever taken but I know it's only empty threats I'm making. I'm blustering.

'Don't play with us. We don't like you.'

I'm speaking for myself and Lesego, like I should. I'm on the watch though, ready on my feet. I'm not taking my eyes once off this crazy piece of fat. If I wound up in her hands there'd be trouble. I'd be in some serious deep crap if that one got her paws on me. I know what I'm talking about. Fat chicks don't play. You don't fall in the hands of an ample girl and come out okay. I've seen many dudes at school coming out of it looking like they've been run over by a steamroller. You don't take a chance with this kind unless you've got some serious beef on you. Goodness knows that if Seolo Magang's chubby child should get a hold of my backside the first thing she'll hasten to do will be to grab my head and make it sink between her thighs where it's dank, and pummel my back a thousand times with a fist, biting her bottom lip, while I thrash helplessly in the steel trap of her legs. Let her come to me if she wants it, then I'll kick her kneecaps over the fence. She doesn't attack me. She turns Lesego loose and runs off to her father. The old man's too busy getting himself tanked up to give her attention. She sulks. At last she whispers something in his ear. He searches his pockets, takes out a bundle of keys and hands it to her. She throws Lesego and me a dirty look, knock-knees her way out of our lives and fucks off. I don't like her one bit.

Evening falls. Maitirelo Malehonyane, my favourite dude Mighty, is back again. He wasn't here for lunch but he's here now. His tongue is awash with new tales. He's not his bubbly old self tonight. He looks a little down in the slop bucket. He tells the men his mind is not in Tlhabane tonight but somewhere a great distance off, behind the mountains where the sun rises at noon and sets at night. He says in all his life he's never been as nostalgic as he is tonight.

'I'm telling you, boys. If it wasn't for the witches of that village I'd go back and live there permanently.'

'The witches?'

'Yes. The witches. There's not one village in this whole land that has half as many witches as that village. The whole settlement swarms with them.'

They know he's about to get rolling with another one so they all turn on their seats and pin their eyes on him. He takes his time about it, he always does.

'There's this one guy, Chochwe.' His pupils dilate. He shakes his head. He lifts the bottle and sips with a crinkled nose, as though the malt was some very sour traditional medicine. He grits his teeth to steel up before he removes the lid and opens the kist to dig up mouldy bits and shreds of the past. He continues.

'I tell you, boys, that was one wicked man. He's still alive you know, old as a lump of shit. They never die. I've seen warlocks in my life, hundreds of them, but not one of them comes close to that one. He dreams about your wife and she wakes up struck down with pains like knives in the waist, and she stays bedridden for weeks. He stinks

71

like a whole sack of onions, only baths at midnight on a full moon. He walks into a kraal and oxen faint. People say he's responsible for half the deaths that have taken place in my village in the last ten years, and I believe it. And it's all Magogwe's fault. You see, in that village Magogwe used to be the sole doctor and healer back in the day. He was an old man, the last one in a line of born witch doctors. And then it emerged one day that this man Chochwe who at the time was known as Kgapetla also had the gift to communicate with the forebears. That one was just an ordinary man in the village, common as a dead dog. I don't know how they did but people found about the man's gift. Old Magogwe lost his fame. Less and less feet started coming into his compound. People started consulting the new seer. Tell us about the future, Chochwe. Tell us about rain. Tell us about our God. He didn't have bones to throw, that's why they called him Chochwe. But they say he had terrific visions and his prophesies were always on the mark. Magogwe didn't like it. He plotted revenge, and he got it. It happened one day at a gathering called by the chief. All the elders were called to *kgotla*, and Magogwe himself being the eldest witch doctor. There was a lot happening, a whole series of ills and evils striking that village at once. Women getting ravished, cattle dying by the hundred, infants that could barely walk disappearing without a spoor, healthy young men kicking the crock at the height of their virility. There was clearly something going on, something not right. Magogwe was asked to throw his bones. He would never pass up an opportunity like that. He invoked the names of a thousand stone-old gods. He intoned a mantra, getting more and more in the spirit as he did. He belched. He squirmed. He whimpered. The bones had spoken, and the witch doctor relayed his findings to the chief. The gods were angry. There was an evil woman in the village. He dropped obscure hints about who it was. He told the chief he could take care of it, but needed the permission of the *kgotla*. The chief gave him his blessings, with the sanction of the whole cabinet, to do what he needed to do. And that was that. They got on their feet and dispersed. And so it happened that the next day one woman in the village could not get up. She was flat on the floor, dead as a carcass. The crone happened to be Kgapetla's mother, the same fellow they called Chochwe. She was on the floor the whole day, the dead woman, her mouth wide open, beetles crawling in and out feasting on the rot stuck between her teeth. That's how her son found her. He did not shed one tear. He buried her alone. He spent the whole afternoon digging a pit, and then he let her go under without a funeral. And then he picked his way back home. He went into his house and didn't come out for a week. He came out one afternoon after nine full days in solitary confinement. It was time to face the sun again. He circumnavigated the village two times, first clockwise, and then counterclockwise. Well some say he did it once, others say he did it three times. Then he went back into his house, at noon, and locked himself in. Tragedy hit the very next morning, and it was no surprise that the witch doctor was the recipient of the first curse. Magogwe went into his kraal as usual to get milk from his milk cows. He was busy working on the udder of the tamest of these when the beast lost it. It spun around in circles like a whirlwind, kicking, bellowing, raising the dead. He waved a stick, the old man, dumbstruck. He gabbled the names of his father's forefathers, pissing himself. The fits left the animal and it turned to face him, and the look in its eye was as ominous as death. It careered into him, and he turned to his heel looking to flee. There was no space. The animal cornered its master and pushed its horns into his breast. His ribs splintered like firewood. The horns pierced right through his breast into his lungs. He bawled like a hippopotamus being slaughtered. That was the end of him. He breathed his last pasted against the kraal, and in that fashion Chochwe had avenged his mother. But that did not mollify him one bit. He went on the rampage. People perished like gnats. People left the village and fled for their lives. I'm not going back there as long as he's still alive.'

'You skipped because of him?' asks one of the men who are too enthralled by Mighty's narration to notice that Lesego and I have crept in close and are also listening.

'No, man. Not really. Something else happened.'

'Ehe? What happened?'

'You see, I was not a problem child growing up. I was meek as a horse; it's a fact. But I did not grow up alone. I grew up with my cousins, and other boys. I was always in trouble, and most of the time it was for stuff I didn't even start. My folks passed on when I was only a bed-wetting tot so I was raised by my uncle. He had livestock like flies, sheep and cattle. He looked after them himself, alone. But during school holidays he went on leave and let us relieve him. There were three of us, his two boys and me. So it was the norm. We were either at school or we were shepherds. He had a massive kraal in his compound, a large *matlhaku* kraal with different compartments for adult animals and their infants. He taught us the whole thing well. We brought the animals back home everyday after a long day out in the woods and knew exactly how to get them back in. We started with the cattle, the adults first. When all of them were in and their gate was bolted we ushered in the calves. The little shits always took us a bit of time, a lot more time than their parents. We needed to keep the calves and their mothers separate all night, everyday, or the udders would be empty as nuts come daybreak, and that old man would skin us. Sheep never gave us crap. My uncle would wake up very early, before everybody, and take to the kraal with two large buckets to get the yield of the milk cows. He'd then open the gates of the different stables and let the young and the old come together and mingle, thus allowing the small ones the opportunity to fill their animals' bellies with their mothers' milk. I wondered sometimes if every young calf knew who its mother was and could recognise them in a crowd, or if the fuckers attacked the first set of teats that came into sight. After filling up the buckets my uncle would come into the house and wake us. We'd go to the small hut behind the big house, boil water and cook porridge. The two fellows, my cousins, would each draw a fresh jug from the buckets and pour over their porridge. I always preferred the previous day's milk, souring milk. I liked the curds. My uncle was an impatient man. We ate quickly. When we finished our food we'd go to my uncle and tell him we were done and ready to start out. He'd get on his spindly shanks and dodder back to the kraal. Back in there he'd march around with the point of his chin on his breastbone, intoning prayers, mingling with the animals like he was one of them, going out of his way to pat every last one of them on the back.'

'Since I was the youngest I was always entrusted with the care of sheep as sheep were easy to look after. There weren't too many head of sheep. My cousins Bomang and Mokuru looked after the cattle. My uncle would open the gates and the animals would shuffle out of the kraal in a file. He'd stand at the gate, the old man, and see to it that none of the small lambs escaped, waving his stick. Then they'd come together, the sheep and the cattle, and the boys and I would slowly drive them out the village into the forest. We always took the same route, the same one Malome taught us. There was always a point where the ovine would separate themselves from the bovine. And so it would be my cue to separate myself from the fellas and stalk the wool. I never really walked after the sheep all day to see to it that they were grazing and not being torn apart by wolves, which in all honesty is the responsibility I was charged with as the shepherd. I spent most of the time perching on treetops, flaying the wind with a whip, humming songs that had no end. It was only once during the day that I would touch down, find the wool and drive them to the river for a drink.'

'I was sitting under a tree one day, my spine propped up against the trunk, minding my own business, when Mokuru came dragging a sheep by the neck. I heard noises of hooves and feet slipping and gripping in the undergrowth and a sheep bleating, crying for help. I got a huge scare, peed myself a little before I hurried to investigate and found it was that cousin of mine. The first thing that sprang to mind had been that a thief was stealing the sheep, and I had no idea how I was going to stop the son of a bitch when I was so skinny and didn't even have a knobkerrie. I steeled myself up and rushed to check what was happening, and that's when I caught Mokuru peeling off his pants. He saw me standing there gawping at him. That immobilised him for a second, but did not deter him. He was on top of something and he was getting on with it. I didn't pretend I wasn't looking either. What happened next shocked me to within a whisker of death. The animal looked as flabbergasted as me, the same sheep that had stopped bleating since it was all a waste of energy. Soon he was naked as the day his mother ejected him, my cousin Mokuru Malehonyane, from the waist down. He kept his shirt on. His organ was huge and circumcised, black as a cinder. The sheep was docile. He pushed its head into a small space between two stems of trees. He did the whole thing with so much precision and so much polish it started to look like he'd done it a few times before. He bent his knees and yanked the tail up in the air. Then he drove his black gonads into the slimy region that was pink as a watermelon. He started jigging and I didn't even hear one song playing. It was astonishing to watch. I had never seen anything like it. The more he bopped the more he gained momentum. The sheep started to laugh. The whole spectacle was sick. He bent his knees another notch and started to go faster. He started making noises, uttering and sputtering senseless things in an unknown tongue. At last he crashed into the animal's hairy hindquarters and didn't come out again. He stood like that for a long time, clinging on to the ewe that was in no hurry to shake him off, like the sheep was a huge magnet and he was a cheap earring. His face dripped with sweat. He pulled himself out, an eternity later, and threw himself to the ground. He lay on his back and spread his legs wide apart, panting, not giving a shit that I was right there watching.'

'It didn't take him forever to recover, and when he did he got on his feet, put on his pants and underpants without beating off the dust on his legs. He released the sheep that turned and sashayed proudly back into the woods, a new spring in its ovine step. He looked at me, shameless as a whore. For a while it looked like he wanted to say something, but he kept mum and said nothing. He turned around and trotted off back to his section of the woods. I waited long enough, and started moving as soon as I was convinced he'd really vamoosed. The sheep had barely covered ground when I pounced on it. The ovine dumbo was still wandering about, alone, looking for its kind. I grabbed it by the neck and dragged it back to where Mokuru had it earlier. I pushed its hornless head back between the stems. I was a newbie at that kind of thing and I had to exercise great caution. I looked around to see if Mokuru had not got clever and decided to lurk about the trees to watch me fall like a fool into his trap. It didn't feel like there was anybody watching so I got down to it. I pulled my pants and underpants down to my ankles and went in. I yanked up the tail like I'd seen my cousin do. I had no skill. I was rough as a brute, from the word pump. I didn't take it one step at a time and gain momentum gradually like Mokuru had done. My enemy was inexperience. I don't think the animal liked me much. I'm sure it found me too much of an amateur. For one thing it didn't burst out laughing like it had done when Mokuru was peppering it earlier. Those corridors were on fire, no wonder Mokuru had sweated so much. The fact that the animal in whose fiords I played did not enjoy me much did not dispirit me one bit. The curiosity was too intense, the madness too wild to curb. I upped my pace a notch and felt the muscles of my thighs stiffen into woody strips. I stretched my legs wide like a giraffe drinking. It was gradual in coming, but in a moment I felt a large stone of pleasure rupture in my kidneys like a seed in hot ash. I put my hands around my pate. I stepped out of my underwear, going full force for the last kill. I went one better than Mokuru, peeled my shirt off my trunk that was basted in sweat. There was no stopping me. I felt like I was giving birth, like I was spawning a hundred scorching eggs. I passed out. When I came to I was on my back, naked as a dog, and nowhere to be seen was the sheep. I shot up quickly and put on my clothes. The slime had dried on me, in my hands, on my crotch, on my legs and on my tummy. There was still a bit of sunshine but it was quite late. I ran helter-skelter through the woods, combing the thicket for the wool. I found them all in one piece, and I could not even tell that one apart from the mob. There was no time. I cracked a whip and started to drive them back home.'

He has been at it for a while, Maitirelo Malehonyane. His throat has begun to creak like a wheelbarrow. He takes time out to grease up. He gropes, grabs a bottle and lifts it to his mouth. He downs the potion in quick loud gulps. I realise for the first time that he is quite an old man, Maitirelo Malehonyane, perhaps even older than my dad. Somewhere out in the busy night a choir of teenage youths, girls, bursts out in song. They sing the chorus of the song declared song of the year by the local radio station; the kind of tune that one either likes or abhors, that plays hour in and hour out on radio and that every tavern has in its jukebox. Some male voice, and a drunken one to boot, waits for an opening, and when the chorus tails off yells: '*Difebe. Difebenyana.* Go to sleep and spare your tiny openings from what hasn't stung them yet.' They ignore him. The chorus goes on and on. There's total silence in this compound for a moment, while Mighty gets himself fuelled up. Their eyes are fast on him, waiting patiently for his tongue to start running again. His thirst is mighty. He drinks the bottle to the butt and nobody complains. He belches, goes again.

'I don't know what happened to me but I lost my head. I had never experienced anything like it before. I couldn't help but crave more of the same. I went into the woods everyday and felt like I was walking into a large harem full of uncomplaining whores, ready to dole out their thanks to the master, in kind. The sheep became my ring of concubines. I was not interested in the girls back in the village anymore. They made a brother graft too hard. Everyday I left home with my cousins and we got to the point where we split, and I did not waste time but picked one and helped myself. The ecstasy of it got bigger and sweeter every time. Mokuru was a genius. The man had unlocked a cave of thrills and left the door open for me. I never caught him at it again but I knew he was sly as a snake. He had probably done it all his life. Well, he never caught me. Every night in the covers I spent the first couple of hours picking fleece from my pubes, fantasising about what I was going to get up to the next day. I owned the woods. Every morning my uncle stamped into the kraal and made conversation with his gods, but not even the spirits knew what I was getting up to.'

'But I got greedy. That kind of thing makes you stupid. You see, the days were getting shorter. There were only a few days to go before schools reopened. I wasn't finding sheep interesting anymore. I wanted something more wild, something by which to round off the holidays in style. It hit me, right on the second last day. I leaped down off the tree on which I had been perched racking my brains. Mokuru had trespassed once and messed with my wool. Well, I was getting one back. It took me a while to get there. I had to be sly. I couldn't just emerge from the meadows, brazen as a jackal, and start chasing the animals around. I was targeting the young ones, the heifers. I took my time in the grass, combing the whole place from the east to the west. When I was convinced my cousins were nowhere in the vicinity I stepped out of the grass and pounced. Cattle were not as cheap as sheep so I needed to be very cunning. It took me a while to catch my bird, a shimmering brown heifer with patches on the neck. I grabbed it by the ear and dragged it off from the group. I led the animal into the designated section of the sheep, and straight to the regular slaughterhouse. We reached the place eventually, the bovine virgin and I, and getting its head caught between the stems was a mission. The child of a bovine hag put up some serious resistance and it took me a bit of time to win that part of the battle. The little shit was feisty as hell. I should have had a rope handy to bind the hindlegs tight together. I hadn't brought a rope obviously, because the idea had come to me not the previous night but just a few minutes before. Anyway, I had got the fat head between the stems so I had to make it snappy. I undressed quickly. Mollo-wa-Kgakala the heifer was not as short as the sheep and I had a bit of difficulty hitting the nest. I stood on my toes and I still failed to get there. It was all very frustrating. That's when I lost it. Time was not on my side, and I was not letting that one escape the injection. I had to try something. I went down and filled my hands with the fetlocks of the hindlegs, and spread them wide apart. Thought it was a great idea, and it could have been had it not been for the little shit losing it. The angle was right and I was about to have a stab when disaster struck. The animal had had enough of the monkey tricks, and I think the stems between which its head was stuck were hurting its neck too. It sprang into the air with hindlegs outstretched. The left hoof caught me full on the yolk sac and I blacked out.'

'It was later in the day when I returned to consciousness to find Bomang and Mokuru hovering over me. I was naked. Bomang was infuriated. The heifer was gone. He threatened to make me walk naked back to the village. He tore a thorny twig off a tree and was about to start flogging my backside with it when Mokuru stood up for me and stopped him. Mokuru pretended to be shocked by the whole thing but said to his older brother 'what the hell, Bomang *monna*, give the *bliksem* his clothes and let's get out of here.' Bomang gave me back my clothes and went and stood at a distance from me, like I stank or something. It was time to go home. I struggled to get on my feet. There was so much pain in my crotch it was a miracle I was still alive. My whole body ached. And that was not even half the story. My groins had swollen to the size of an egg of an ostrich. Bomang was on the verge of tears. He told me to my face that I was on my own. He was disgusted beyond consolation, and I wondered if he'd never in his life got up to mischief or done something stupid. His attitude made me want to throw up. Mokuru was better, more understanding. He was, after all, my mentor, my partner in crime. I wondered if he had also once upon a time been kicked on the bonnet by an animal, and with as much punch as I was kicked. He was far too understanding.'

'We got home later than usual because I was walking very slowly. Anyway we needed to take our time and come up with a story we were going to give the grown-ups, for they were sure going to pick it up that I was hurt. We could not tell them the truth so we needed to have the same story to tell. It took us a while to agree on one thing, mainly because that Bomang wanted no part in the whole thing. All he wanted to do was be a good kid and tell the truth. Mokuru begged him for a long time to see reason, and he came around eventually. In the end we all agreed that the story we were going to give the folks back home was that I'd stepped on a stone chasing after a straying sheep, and lost my footing and sprained my knee bad. Bomang was broody all the way back home, keeping quiet as a secret. Only once did he try to reach out. He squatted on the ground and offered to carry me on his back. It was too painful. My swollen knackers got sandwiched between my crotch and his horny back and the pain was excruciating. I tried to be brave but could not keep myself from whimpering. He got pissed and put me down, cussing like a bitch.'

'We got home and my uncle was there to receive us, to receive his livestock actually. I saw the man and knew at once that I had to man up, or else. I held the pain in and made an effort to move as normally as possible. His wife dished up for us and we feasted in silence. At least my appetite was still intact. The pain was still there, more intense than before. I was not going to be a baby. I had after all incurred my injury from a disgraceful act. I went to bed hoping things would be better the next morning. I went into the house before I turned in and stole some of the ointment that my aunt trusted very much and had used on me when I had had minor accidents in the past. I smeared the unguent thick all over my groins and conked out.'

'The morning came too soon. My head had not been in the pillow for more than a few hours when my uncle was back in the hut shaking us out of sleep. Bomang was the first to come to. His father told him to wake us and left our hut. The first thing I did that day was put my hand in my drawers. The discovery I made was not nice.'

He pauses again to have another bite at the bottle, but this time he's not at it for more than a few seconds. He continues as smoothly as though he hadn't paused at all.

'My knackers were swollen, hard as a whetstone, round as an udder. I sweated. My brow ached. I knew I was in trouble. I was still lying supine in my shakedown. I pressed my hands into the mattress and tried to lift my upper body. When I had passed the first challenge and I was sitting upright I tried to push myself to get up on my feet. I couldn't. A bolt of pain hit me. I fell back on my back and hit the mattress with a thud. My head spun, my ears whistled. I panicked. The old man was outside waiting for us to come and take the animals out to the woods to graze. I didn't know what to do. I remembered the salve under my pillow and reached for it, dug out a gob and applied it on the swelling. I was desperate. I started to massage the swelling, anxious to get on my feet and get going. The pain was wild. Bomang was on his feet calling out orders. He had forgotten about my accident, but Mokuru hadn't. His eyes surveyed me with a lot of concern. I tried to stand up again, and the same thing happened.'

'"I can't. I can't stand up, man. It's too painful," I told my cousin Mokuru Malehonyane.'

'I started to weep. Bomang was outside peeing with a fresh penis and scratching his cojones, waiting for Mokuru and me to come out and take on another day. He waited for us for a while and we did not come out, so he came looking for us. He found Mokuru hovering over me, inspecting my nether region. The sight of the black balloon between my legs knocked him back.'

'"Shit. I forgot about this shit's balls. Damn you, man, see what mess you've put us all in? I'm coming clean before you die. I'm going to tell the old folks what happened and don't you dare deny it or I'll kill you before this swelling does. I told you, we should have come clean last night. We wouldn't be in all this shit right now." He was mad.

Mokuru tried to reason with him but he was having none of it this time. Mokuru told him that I was not going to die, that he should think twice about the thing and all possible repercussions before he went ratting. He'd heard it all before, Bomang Malehonyane, the gangling firstborn child of my uncle and aunt's haunches. He was coming clean. As far as he was concerned I deserved all that was coming, a little more even. He flew out of the hut like a paper aeroplane thrown from the back of a classroom all the way to the blackboard by a stupid child who is certain as hell that he is not going to pass come final exams and does not give a shit about it. It was quiet for a while and my heart was beating like a drum. Mokuru's eyes were large and about to pop out of his skull, and then my aunt's honk rose above the quiet of the morning to punch holes in the sky. My uncle did not cry out in shock but came dashing into the hut like a bull. He bent over me like Mokuru had done and pulled the blanket off that I had taken cover under. My aunt and Bomang were already in the hut when the old bull came breathing down on me after throwing the blanket to the roof. The second time around he angrily and shamelessly forced my legs apart, like he was about to help me deliver a baby or make love to me. He ripped my underpants off my waist. He was ruthless as hell in the act of undressing me, so reckless that the elastic waistband of the underpants brushed against my swollen pouch and I screamed with pain. "Shut up!" he cried. He retreated a few inches to study the injury from a distance. My aunt saw the swollen balloon for the first time and almost passed out. She put her arms on her mouth as if to vomit out all the disbelief into them. She cried. My uncle was enraged. He wanted to make me lie on my stomach and flay my buttocks with a wire, and I was lucky my aunt was there to bail me out. "You can't do that to the child,

Papa." "Child? Child, huh? This thing's not a child but a lump of shit, a bloody curse. I want him out of my home by sunset."'

'My uncle was mad and I kind of understood. I cast a helpless glance at Mokuru and he begged me not to rat on him. I was not a chick. I was not like that son of a bitch Bomang. I understood. Mokuru's secret was safe with me. I was knee-deep in crap. The man had just said that he was kicking me out. That was a fix and a half, I'm telling you. Where was I to go? My aunt stormed out of the hut and into the big house and returned with a basket full to the brim with unguents. Breaking into tears was the only thing that made sense at that point. My throat was dry as concrete. My uncle's wife knelt by my side and got busy applying the ointments on my swollen parts. She rubbed and massaged, was at it for about ten minutes. There was nothing more she could do so she told me to stay in bed for a while. She got up on her feet, grabbed her pail of ointments and left me alone in the hut. My cousins had already left with their father because the old man was not taking chances no more. His livestock was precious to him. The prospect of not seeing that old man the whole day brought me an amount of relief. My aunt came back to the hut about an hour later, bearing porridge and unguents. She promised me that she would get my uncle to extend my stay by another week at least. She was not prepared to push Letlhakore any farther than that. She told me that she hoped that I would have recuperated satisfactorily in a week. I was ashamed of myself and I was thankful that my aunt had gone against the current of the old man's fury and got me cut some slack. I found a lot of solace in her support.'

'"Mma Malome, I'm sorry I tried to rape the calf. It was a disgraceful deed. I don't know what came over me."'

'My statement embarrassed her more than it embarrassed me. She didn't say a word but sat quietly by my side rubbing the balloon with a cloth that every now and then she dunked in steaming water that she'd brought in in a tub. Keletso came in, my uncle's youngest child. She came into the hut and came and hovered over us, and her mother did not chase her out. She saw me there, flat on my back like a corpse, her mother massaging my privates. Her eyes swelled instantly with curiosity. She had never seen a penis before, and there was hardly any penis to see that time. The balloon was large and round and black and shiny, and my organ looked like a small little finger appended to it. The old woman nursed me patiently. I felt the pain getting less intense. She dried her hands with the hem of her dress. She put away the ointments and the swab, took my hand and helped me to my feet. She coddled over me like a mother. She was amazing.'

'I got dressed and stepped out of the hut for the first time that day. The sun had been up for a long time. There was still a bit of pain in the injured region, but nothing like what I felt earlier. I stayed on my feet, moving. I did not want to look like a sissy in front of my aunt and her little girl. I stammered out to the toilet, watched by the clouds. I got to the toilet that I realised for the first time was very far from the house. I got inside, pulled my pants down to my knees as though preparing to rape a sheep. I trained the small little appendix into the hole of the toilet and pushed. The trickle came and all my aunt's work came undone. It felt like a small intestine was being pulled out of my bladder. I didn't know what to do. I was only a poor orphan and surely the loss of my folks had been enough of a misfortune. I was dying. I could already see a grave, a narrow, deep pit crawling with worms even before my body was interred in it. I held an emergency conference with myself and decided that I didn't care anymore. I was ready for whatever lay on the horizon. I pushed again, and my dilution felt like splinters of wood when it left my system. It was terrible. I felt like a blacksmith was pinning my waist bone against an anvil and beating it to powder. I finished peeing and walked back to the hut with steady steps like nothing had happened. Time passed and I healed. The old bastard lugged me out of the hut the day before I left and made me finger the calf I had attempted to ravish. Of course I had not forgotten which one it was. It was embarrassing, but I named and shamed the bitch. He went into the kraal with a spear, and two minutes later Mollo-wa-Kgakala the heifer was on the floor, dead as an ant. The day dawned. I had no money and my aunt out of the goodness of both her purse and her heart gave me three brown notes. My uncle did not like it one bit. With tears in my eyes and shame in my voice I said goodbye to my aunt and young Keletso who surely got chicken skin when she recalled what she saw a couple of days earlier. She had surely not forgotten. I wished I could call her to one side and open my clothes and show her that it wasn't that bad anymore. I said goodbye lastly to my partner in wrongdoing, Mokuru. My mentor. He was genuinely sad to see me leave, but he was mostly relieved that I had not ratted on him. I took the punch alone for both of us and I'm sure he respected me for it. My uncle had contrived to be out when I made my exit. I don't know why I chose the place but I got in a taxi and took out to Klerksdorp. I had never been there before, not once in my life. There I slept in parks and did this and that for survival and slowly picked my way to Rustenburg. Life is a fucker when you're an orphan, boys. It is the worst thing in the world coming of age without a parent in the world. You're alone. In the cold. In rain. In sickness. Everyday. The world kicks you around so hard. So hard. You should be glad you never had to go through it. Trust me.'

His eyes fill up with tears. He drinks another bottle to the bottom and struggles to his feet. He peels himself away from the crowd and goes and stands in the far corner. He is very emotional right now. I feel sorry for him. Such a cool guy. I take Lesego by the hand and take her home, feeling very sad, and then I come back home and go to bed.

I wake up early. Thursday, December the 26th. The Day of Goodwill. The last official public holiday on the South African almanac. I sit in front of the box and watch a kids' variety show presented by a fair little thing whose looks and mannerisms remind me very much of Lesego. I wolf a red apple down to the stone. The old people come crawling out of stuffy bedrooms like insects. The women plunge into the task of cleaning and I go outside to sit by myself on the lawn. The hours scream by quickly and before we know it it's a few minutes past three in the afternoon. My father and Malome Jobe tell my mom and my aunt that they will be hanging out at Spirits' place tonight, at the old man's request. Spirits asked them because he didn't want to leave his little girl on her own back at his house. The wives give their permission and the husbands get on their way.

I realise for the first time tonight how much I enjoy the company of the old men. Their absence has certainly left a great black hole on the atmosphere. I haven't seen Lesego the whole day. I don't see her tonight either. I walk up and down the street in the style of her father on his first day here. She doesn't come out of the house. I sit for an hour outside the gate until I get tired. The next day is equally boring. My dad has gone back to work and Malome Jobe's not home the whole day. My father returns from work and they set out to Spirits' place again tonight. This time I have enough presence of mind not to go and waste my time standing at the gate like a guard.

Saturday the 28th. I wake up to find everybody up. My father tells me to pack my bag, tells me he's taking me on a trip to the bundus.

'I'm taking you to meet your grandparents, son.'

'My grandparents? You're taking me today?'

'Pack enough clothes for two weeks. You're coming back in the new year.'

He says it's been too long since he last saw his people. My body quivers with exhilexcitement. My mother once told me that the last time my grandparents saw me I was about fourteen months old. Of course I can't remember a thing about it. I have been alive for a decade and I have never seen my grandparents, and that my old man is about to take me to them is as thrilling as anything.

'What should I take, Papa?'

'I don't know, Prof. Ask your mother. I think two pairs of shoes and enough clothes should be fine.'

'What about my toothbrush?'

'Yes. And underpants.'

I am first in the bath. I wash quickly, and then it's my dad's turn. He never wastes time in there. Mom helps me pack to make sure I take everything. When the bags are packed and my dad and I are ready to hit the road we do just that. My mom has packed my stuff in her small suitcase that moves on wheels. My dad does not lug the case but takes it by the handle. He hasn't packed a bag for himself. Mom has put a clean shirt and clean underpants for him in my suitcase, and a bag of toiletries.

We get to the taxi rank at about 10 o'clock. My enthusiasm bombs when the queue marshal points us to our taxi. It is an old square tin with tattered seats and plays some radio station that plays a lot of horrible music with a sound that is not very clear. We find a skinny woman inside who must be twenty-nine or thirty. The whole taxi smells like a restaurant, and that is because the woman has a pack of greasy fries on her lap and is scoffing them down, and right above her crown is a large sticker with the words NO EATING in bold. Why people ever eat in the taxi is beyond me. There are three of us in this old crate that according to yet another sticker is certified to carry fifteen passengers. The wait for more people proves to be a lot of excruciating hell. It must be thirty-five minutes since my dad and I boarded when five people consult the queue marshal and he points a finger at the old tin. About time. Or not. The joy of more people coming is short-lived though, because the dolts get to the cab and only one of them is travelling. The rest stand at the door and wait until he's settled, then they say farewell and saunter off back into town.

The marathon continues. Three more people have hopped on but we still need nine more for this thing to get moving. We've been here for almost two hours, and there's still only the four of us in the cab. This must be the longest that my dad has been without a drink in his hand all year, not being at work. And we wait and wait, and wait and wait some more. The whole thing gets even more frustrating when people start coming through but refuse to board the transport. 'We know this old thing. It will have broken down four times by the time it gets to Sannieshof.' 'I know. I'd rather walk than get aboard this piece of shit. Last year I missed Chwaro's funeral because of it.' And so they stand outside and wait for the next one. The waiting crowd outside grows until there are more people outside than inside the taxi, and soon there's a full load of fifteen people waiting for a better and more trustworthy vehicle to take them home to Delareyville, and Vryburg. Two fools that have grown tired of waiting for our taxi to get full grab their bags and get out of the old tin to join the waiting bunch. The queue marshal comes to the party and tries to reason with the rebels to get inside the taxi. They refuse. He begs them till his tongue is green but they won't budge.

'Come on, guys. It's quarter-past twelve. There's no chance in the world you'll get home late. Come on.'

'We're not interested, brother. Just take this thing off our line already. Give us better transport.'

He's done begging. He turns on the aggro.

'You wanna be difficult, eh? You wanna be clever? Fine. You'll stand here roasting all day. If you don't wanna get into this one you won't get into the next three taxis. It's a promise. I'll see to it. I have no time for people like you. I'm going nowhere. Not me. I'll be here all day.'

Two or three are moved, grab their bags and get in, the bulk of the crowd remains unmoved. It would appear they've heard the same threats one too many times before.

'He does not have a taxi. He won't stop me.'

My old man and I have been in here for nearly four hours when the last passenger comes in and the door is shut. The queue marshal comes with a clipboard and passes it around for all passengers to write their names and addresses. My dad puts down false names and addresses for himself and for me and hands the clipboard to the guy sitting next to us. I ask him why later and he tells me it is because he was pissed off with the whole wait. He says he thinks it's a stupid idea anyway. An old man with the face of a newborn child jumps into the driver's seat, puts on a cassette and gets the engine running.

My father has warned me that we're in for an excruciating long trip and I've braced myself.

'Why now, Papa?'
    'Huh?'
    'Why did you decide to take me now to meet my grandparents?'
    'Oh. Look, Prof, it's something a friend of mine said the other day. I'm very uncouth, son. I don't always do the right thing. Look, family's important. I don't want you to miss out on a chance to get to know your grandparents because of my recklessness.'
    'Okay. So why's Mom not coming with us?'
    'Somebody has to stay behind and look after the house, son. Besides, your mom has to go to work.'
    'Are we going to meet your parents or Mom's parents, Papa?'
    'My parents, Prof. Your mother's parents have both passed away. They passed away six years before you were born, two months apart.'

'What happened?'
'They were sick.'

Tears fill my eyes. I never knew. I feel sorry for Mom, belatedly. It must have been very hard for her. I put up an effort to keep back the tears but my dad notices my sudden sadness. He gives me an assuring squeeze on the shoulder.

'It's okay, son. It was a long time ago.'

The road is indeed very long. The distance between Rustenburg and Koster, the first town we pass, is mighty, but the old tin's performance is terrific. It overtakes small cars and flies over potholes and my attitude towards it changes significantly. We're between Lichtenburg and Sannieshof, as my father tells me, when a traffic cop gets in front of the crate and signals to the driver to pull over. They ask for a permit. The old man with a child's face hands them a document that he retrieves from the sunshield that he has had turned up since we left Rustenburg. The officers say something to one another that only they and our driver can hear. Our driver smiles and all seems to be well. They ask for his driving licence and he gives it to them. They look it over. They give our guy the green light and we're on the tarred road again. We make Delareyville in three hours and the taxi dumps me and my dad in a quiet street. The man with a child's face kicks it on to Vryburg and I have to hold myself from patting him on the back and telling him how terrific he's been. Delareyville is a pretty small town. Not necessarily too small compared to Rustenburg but still quite small. My dad tells me the town hasn't changed one bit since he was hereabouts growing up.

'Is there a cinema in this town, Papa?'

'I don't know, son. When I was growing up we never watched any movies.'

'Really?'

'Uh-huh.'

'What did you do?'

'I don't know. I can't remember. It was a long time ago.'

'You herded sheep?'

'Don't be silly. My father was a pauper.'

We check into a busy restaurant, at my father's lead, and place an order at the counter. We order two plates of pap and steak and tear into our orders as soon as they're plonked on our table. My dad orders two quarts of beer for himself and a litre of orange juice for me. We finish our food quickly and gulp down our drinks. Now we set out to get to the end of our trip. My dad takes us to the supermarket where we stock up on sweets and fruit and three six-packs of fizzy drinks. We go back to the restaurant and my dad buys a packet of chips and two loaves of white bread. He's got too much in his hands so I help him with two plastic bags. They're heavy as hell, the two bags, but I'm not going to tell him or my dad will think I'm a sissy. There comes a time when a brother's gotta man up and this is one of those. We get to the taxi rank and board a taxi to take us to my old man's cradle. At least we don't wait very long for the taxi to get full this time. A few minutes in and we're moving. We go out of town and into a wilderness. There is so much dust behind us where our taxi has passed it's hard to believe we're travelling on a tarred road and not a dirt one. We make the village late in the afternoon. The taxi stops once for a skinny teenager that wears a cap back to front to touch down. It proceeds a small distance into the village and my father calls it to another stop. We touch down and the driver kicks it away.

The village looks like nothing I had in mind. We walk through a long street that is not as straight as the streets back in my township but snakes like a footpath. In front of every house there sits a mob of people and I wonder if they're members of the same families. My father spins his pumpkin head from one side of the street to the other, greeting folks he has not seen in a long time. Everyone seems to recognise him still. One of the ladies that sits before a house that we pass can't believe her eyes when she sees my father.

'*Batho*, Masimong. You're still alive? Somebody told us you died. Your mother shaved her head and mourned for six months.'

'You should know better than to believe such crap.'

'Your mother believed it.'

'Don't be stupid, woman. My mother never believed that shit.'

It is not long before we fork into one of the houses that line the snaking street. My dad opens the gate and we step in.

'Son, we're home,' he tells me. We step up to the front door and he knocks once. He turns the handle and steps inside when nobody answers. An old woman meets up with us halfway into the house and her hands go up in the air. She gropes for a chair, plonks herself down, covers her mouth with her hands and casts her eyes out the window into the distance. She brings back her eyes and we're still here. Something in her head splits. She starts to weep. They come gushing out her system, tears of shock, like a tempest. She's at it for a while, moaning with emotion, and my dad does nothing. There is no rush. We wait for her. The gale of her emotions subsides and she wipes her snot and her tears with a handkerchief that she pulls out from the pocket of her frock.

'Masimong?'
    'It's me, Ma. It's me.'
    'Why, Masimong? Why?'
    'It's okay, Ma. I'm here.'

The old woman, my grandmother, has stopped crying. I don't know how we wound up here but we're in the living room. My grandmother lifts her chin and our eyes meet. I avert my face. Her eyes are red as a stop sign.

'Is it true that they said I was dead, Ma?'
    'Yes.'
    'And you believed them?'
    'I always knew you'd return, Masimong. I never believed any of that rubbish.'

My grandmother now turns her attention to me.

'Masimong, is this child who I think he is?'

My dad nods. The old woman's eyes well up with tears again, but this time she does well to keep the emotions in check.

'Leungo? Is it you, child? Come here. Come to Grandma.'

She takes me in her bosom and gives me the firmest hug ever. She strokes my head. She kisses my brow. She seems very happy to be reunited with me. Two youngsters come into the house through the front door while my grandma and I are still bonding. Twins. About six years of age.

'Come on in, boys,' says Grandma. 'Come meet your cousin.'

'Who are they?' asks my father.

'Phenyo and Phitlhelelo,' replies Grandma. 'Salang's boys. There is another one that I know you know, their elder brother Diepeng.'

My grandmother's words have barely dried when a youngster that's not much older than me comes stamping into the house. He wears a short-sleeved checked shirt inside out, unbuttoned, and a pair of short navy-blue pants. His legs are covered in dust from the knees right down to the bare toes. He's been out all day, playing in the sun.

'This is him, Diepeng,' Grandma tells my dad. 'Diepeng, come, child, and say hello to your uncle Masimong and your cousin Leungo. They've come back from the dead.'

The twins are not shy. They close in on him and start getting friendly with my dad.

'They're Salang's boys, all three of them. Your father and I would be alone in the world if we didn't have these boys.'

'Speaking of the old man, where is he, Ma?'

'He's under the covers sleeping.'

'Sleeping? So early? In this heat?'

'Your father does not know the difference anymore. He sleeps any time. He's not a young man anymore, you know. But you're right. He must come out here and see you. Diepeng, go wake your grandfather, child. Tell him his son is here.'

The boy rushes off, returns a few minutes later to tell Grandma that the old man refuses to wake up.

'Did you tell him his son is here?'
    'Yes, Grandma.'
    'And what did he say?'
    'He says he has no son.'

Grandma decides to get on her feet and go fetch her husband herself. She's gone for a long time. She returns a few minutes later with the old man in tow. It's him. It's my grandpa. I take one look at him and I know at once that it is him. He looks every inch like his son. He must be in his very late sixties or early seventies, or eighties. With the elderly one can never be fully sure that they're guessing the age alright. Unlike my dad whose head is shaved the elder has a shock of black and white hair on his nut. His beard is longer than my dad's.

'Masimong.'
    'I'm alive, Pa. It's me.'
    'No, you're not. You're not alive, Masimong. Nobody who's alive and well, no grown man with tradition and culture leaves home and stays away for eight years. Only an idiot does something like that, a fool with no principles. An animal. What do you expect us to say now? Huh? That we're elated to see you again? What a waste of space you are. I should have had more children, if only I'd known you'd turn out like this. Why was I dragged out of bed anyway? To come and sit here with you? You've been away for years, surely you could have waited for me for fifteen minutes?'

The old man speaks so slowly he may as well call the punctuation marks out loud. My father lowers his head in shame. His eyes well up. There's so much tension in here even the tots are feeling it. I bet my father could do with a cold one right now. I feel sorry for him. Grandpa's being unfair, giving my dad the treatment and all. This is supposed to be a happy time. If the elder does not go easy on giving him the talking-to my dad will either pass out or burst into tears. The elder seems to read my mind. He quits slating my father. He turns to look at me, my father's old man.

'Look how old his son has grown, and he's been keeping him away from us. I really don't understand the head of my son.'

The elder studies me like a book. He wants to start a conversation, with me, but he doesn't seem to know what to start by saying. So he keeps on staring, poring into me, seeing right through my soul like an X-ray machine. He really has nothing to say to me, nothing just yet. I can't help him. I'm just a kid. What do kids know about starting conversations with people one hundred years older than them? His wrinkled eyelids flicker, and the elder turns his head to turn his attention away from me. He pulls my dad by the nape of the neck and they step outside. They're gone for a long time, my old man and my dad, and I'm left alone with my grandmother and the three boys. I kind of understand where the old people are coming from and I'm angry with my dad too. Grandpa and my dad go outside which gives me an opportunity to look around and check out the place. It is a very shabby house, even for elders. There's clutter everywhere; dust on the clock on the wall. And stains on the curtains. And holes on the sofas. And a musty smell that is as solid in its stance as the walls themselves. The boys won't let me check out the place in peace, the little ones. They come closer. They stand right under my nostrils and gawp at me like I am some magician dishing out tricks. I return the favour and stare right back. These boys are by some distance the ugliest small boys I've ever seen, certainly the ugliest set of twins I've ever laid my eyes on. I want to burst out laughing but I can't. I can't be a savage on my very first day. The boys and I don't exchange words. We get to know each other in silence like that. My dad and Grandpa come back into the house. The elder's anger has subsided. He's even remembered what it was he wanted to say to me earlier.

'Come, grandson. Come sit on my lap.'

I stand up and shuffle forward to his seat, and instead of letting me jump on his legs he exhausts every last bit of energy his elderly life has left and hoists me. He plonks me on his lap, puffing.

'Leungo? Heh? Leungo *la botshelo*. Welcome home, son.'

All I can do is smile. I really am very happy to be in this house with these folks. I feel a sense of belonging like nothing I have ever felt.

It doesn't take me too long to learn that words travel fast in this village, thunder fast. A couple of battered guys knock on the front door and it's barely been an hour since we've arrived. 'We heard you came, Masimong,' they tell my dad. They come in without being invited and sit with us for a while, getting loudly reunited with my old man. And they have no culture either, because they get on their feet a few

101

minutes later and bamboozle my father into hitting the streets with them. This one has no backbone. He pretends like he does not like it one bit but he knows these old louts are doing him a huge favour. He has not gone as long as he did today without a drink in the last ten years. Our bags have already been taken to the room where we will be sleeping, I think by Grandma. The fellow Diepeng leaves the house to go sit under the tree at the back of the house. He doesn't invite me to come with him but I follow him anyway. It is under the tree behind the house where we become friends. It's quite hard to tell what the guy's into. He's a bit of a dull one too. I find out very soon that there isn't a heck of a lot he knows.

'Do you know how to play Roboteq 4, Diepeng?'
   'Eh?'
   'Never mind. Which school do you go to?'
   'The same one that everybody goes to.'
   'And which one is that?'
   'Look, I don't wanna talk about school. Not today.'

He asks how old I am and I tell him twelve, but of course I'm lying. I am only nine years and eleven months old. He tells me he's fourteen and I don't believe him. He looks a little too young to be fourteen, but I don't oppose him. Or maybe he's right. You never know with country folk.

It's been a long day but it has not even started to get dark yet. My dad had a secret caucus with his mother before he stepped out earlier, gave her a couple of blue notes to buy whatever she wanted. The afternoon is starting to wear off very quickly. Grandma calls Diepeng and gives him a note to run to the supermarket to buy a live chicken. Diepeng starts walking, and again I follow him without invitation.

Getting to the shops turns out to be quite a trip, a mission. We get there eventually, and the shop is of some size. It's a supermarket with a silly name on its forehead. Papi Super Trader. Papi must be a retard, if that's somebody's name. Trader is an anagram for retard, anyway. Papi Super Retard. That's more like it.

'Are there arcade games in this shop?'
   'It's a shop, *monna*, not a crèche.'

We don't go into the supermarket but onwards to the back. Then we turn once to the left, to the back of the shop. There there's a man manning a coop full of chickens. Topless. Fat. Rude. His chickens are nothing like the son of a bitch. They're skinny and sickly and enclosed in a pen that is not very clean. The whole place smells like shit. Diepeng doesn't bother checking them individually to pick out the fattest one. This one's bought too many chickens in his life to give a toss about that kind of thing anymore. He crawls inside and attacks them, and grabs the first one he meets. He comes out and shuts the coop, and hands fatty the blue note. The topless one does not like it one bit.

'Dammit man,' he explodes. 'Go around to the shop and ask for change. That's not the kind of money you bring at this time of the day. What is the matter with you?'

Diepeng hands me the sickly bird and dashes around to the shop to ask for change. I hold the little shit at arm's length, far away from my body. It stinks. I don't know why Grandma didn't just send us for braai packs. Diepeng comes back with change. He gives the man a brown note and he swoops it like a thief. He digs in his pockets and gives my cousin change. Our business here is done.

Diepeng gives the signal this time and we get on our way back home. I try to give him back the chicken but he refuses to take it. He says I should carry the bird because I'm younger, because I have never carried a chicken before, and because I'm going to eat it as well. I try to lie to him, tell him I've got an allergy. He buys none of it. I bet he doesn't even know what an allergy is. It has grown quite dark but he can still make his friends out from a distance. When a figure appears he drops his shoulders and lowers his head, and pastes the figure against the sky that is still quite bright, compared to the ground. Then he can tell who the figure is, just like that. 'Oh, it's so-and-so.' He whistles a tune. He picks pebbles and throws them into the night. He somersaults, backflips and sideflips and all of them. He won't take the chicken from me.

'I'll put it down.'
    'I dare you.'

The meal is lovely. Grandma has a terrific hand. I wolf down the meat and try hard not to remember the state the chicken was in in its last minutes in the world of the living. Diepeng and I eat in the living room and watch television at the same time. The twins and Grandpa and Grandma eat in the old people's bedroom. I'm still quite full from the large meal my dad made me eat in the afternoon before we boarded the last taxi to here at that restaurant in Delareyville, but Diepeng is apparently hungry as a dragon and buries his plate in a flash. Grandma's seen it fit to save the two loaves of bread and chips my father bought in Delareyville for tomorrow. I offer Diepeng what I don't have space for and he sweeps it. He's got an appetite like a disease.

'I'll dry,' he says immediately upon burying the last bite.

'What?'

'The dishes. Come. You wash, I dry. That way we finish quicker and we can come back here to watch TV before this movie gets too old. Come.'

'Come on, man. The dishes? I've never washed the dishes in my life.'

'Then you're about to do it for the first time in your life. They won't wash themselves.'

'Yes, I know that. But, dude, I don't live here. Don't be foolish.'

'You're here now. You've just had supper in this house.'

'I know. But I don't live here like full-time. I'm a guest. You can't make a guest wash the dishes.'

He won't take it. He presses a button and the TV goes black. He's worse than my mother. He turns off the light in the living room. He tells me that in his opinion anybody who can hold a spoon and feed himself is totally capable of washing the dishes. I wash and he dries. There's no sink. We do the dishes in a large enamel bowl, on the floor. He makes me scrub the pots. The kitchen is spotless as a spoon when we leave it. And now he's tired, all of a sudden, and he's not going back to the sitting room to watch TV. The little shit deceived me. He calls it a night and takes to his room that he shares with the twins. The twins are already fast asleep on animal skins that Diepeng tells me are called *diphate*.

'Go away, *monna*. I want to sleep.'

'Already?'

'Yes. I told you I was tired.'

He slips under the covers, checked shirt and all, and he has not even bothered to wipe his legs with a wet cloth. Two and a half minutes in and he's already snoring, out cold like a rat on poison. I've seen idiots in my life, but this guy takes the plate hands down. I leave him and his sibs to it. Everybody's gone to bed. The lights are off in the whole house, all but the one in the room my old man and I will be crashing in. I don't bother to go back and check if the front door is locked. I poke my head behind the curtain to look out into the world. This place is dark as death. There's not even one street light out there. It creeps me out staring into the dark like that. I feel like a crooked, long finger could appear any minute out of the black and poke me in the eye. I move away from the window back into the bedroom that apparently belongs to Diepeng and the twins' mom, my aunt Salang who Diepeng told me works in Reivilo and comes home once every two weeks. I've got a choice to make: either crawl in bed and warm the sheets for my dad, or grab one of those skins and crash alone on the floor. I have not slept in a proper bed in a long time, so the choice is quite an easy one. I look around for it but can't find the switch, so I leave the lights on. I take off my shoes, my shirt and my pants, and get between the bedclothes in only my undies. I sleep right on the edge of the bed. I have never slept with my dad in my life, and that I am crashing with him tonight is as uncomfortable as anything. I hope he's not the type that likes to be all touchy-touchy or I'll be seriously pissed with him. He will be in here in a few hours' time, smelling like a brewery. That guy's something else. Next time I come here I'm coming alone, or with my mother. My mom would never have left me behind, alone with strangers. They're my grandparents, sure, but I don't really know these people. My dad must just grow up one day. My head hits the pillow and I'm gone.

I am woken the next morning by a knock on the door of the bedroom. I didn't hear him come in last night but here's my dad next to me, all over the place like a corpse. The person at the door knocks again and I touch down to go and check who it is. It is my grandpa come to wake us up, me and my dad both. He tells me he's taking us to the graveyard.

'Is there a funeral, Grandpa?'

'Don't be ridiculous, child. Where'd you see a tent in this village?'

'So why are we going to the graveyard?'

'Look, I don't like your questions. Now get that father of yours out of that bed.'

Getting Masimong out of the sack is a job. I shake him like a patient. I slap his cheeks repeatedly. I pull him by the ears. I drill a finger into a damp armpit. Nothing. It's when I get pissed and scream in his ear that he finally snaps out of it. He comes out of it with a start. He gets off the bed and dodders past me without greeting me, mumbling, chewing. He comes back, puts on a shirt and sandals, and we hit the footpath, right behind my grandpa's travelling stoop. I've never seen an elder move so swiftly. I have to trot to keep up, and I'm not even fully awake yet.

The graveyard is a vast yard with graves. I don't remember ever being in a place like this. It gives me the chills being here right now, moments before daybreak. Not all of them have tombstones. Grandpa has reduced his speed and we pick our way slowly through the tombs, heaps and heaps of white stone. There's silence all around. My grandfather, our tour guide, takes us from one tomb to the other. I don't know exactly how old this one is but he really has a steady pair of legs for a man his age. At each grave he takes us to he squats and orders that we do the same. Then he starts to utter some kind of speech or prayer, his head on his breast. My dad's name is in there somewhere, and something about a new wave and the elimination of evil. I really can't see why he wanted me out here. I am just here, and I don't even what's going on. He could have just woke my dad and left me alone. I doubt my old man himself knows what's cooking. He's been yawning non-stop ever since we got here, squatting like he's in the toilet and taking a bit of time to get back up on his feet. None of the tombs that Grandpa takes us to has a tombstone or is labelled or has anything with a name on it and I wonder how he knows that they're the right ones, but I don't have the bottle to ask him. We exit the graveyard and we're on our way back home, thirty-something minutes later. The sun has come out and it's already blazing. Either Diepeng or my grandmother has put a small tub at the gate with clean water in it. We wash our hands, leave the tub at the gate and go inside.

My dad washes up and puts on fresh clothes, and only stays for about three hours after breakfast. Then he gets on his feet and kicks off a flurry of goodbyes. He tells me in front of her that he's given my grandmother the money, return fares for when I will be going back to Tlhabane next year, on the eighth of January.

'So I will be here until next year, Dad?'

'Yes, son. I think I did hint that you'll be here for a while. I just forgot to say it in so many words.'

'It's okay, Dad. I'm not complaining.'

He says that Grandma will give the money to me on the

morning of the eighth. Grandma's already folded the notes many times and put them in a safe place.

'You must cut out your nonsense, Masimong. Come home every now and then. You're the only son we've ever had.'
  'I know, Ma. I'll try.'
  'Salang has a cellular phone. You must speak to your sister every now and then. And you must send us money. We've got these kids to looks after. Do you understand?'
  'Yes, Mother.'

Grandpa's not digging the fact that my dad is getting on his way back already. He sulks like a boyfriend, sits quiet and waits for an opening. When the first half-chance to launch the assault donates itself he pounces like a duck.

'You come in today, you go out tomorrow. After so many years, Masimong? What a waste you are.'
'Look, Father, I have a job to get back to. I'll come and visit again soon, I promise.'
  'I'll be dead soon, Masimong. Now you know.'

Grandpa's seriously irritated. He stays behind when the five of us accompany my dad to the main road to catch a taxi. The distance one covers around here to get a cab is ridiculous. It's not even a proper bus stop with a shelter where we stop to wait for the taxi. There's not even a tree to huddle under. We're screwed. We stand in a group under the sun, getting blacker and blacker. Ten minutes go by, and fifteen. Twenty. Half an hour. No taxi. I don't know what's worse, waiting in the taxi for the taxi to get full, or waiting by the roadside for the taxi to come coasting from somewhere. Serves my dad right. If he'd saved half the money he's spent on drinks in the last nine years he'd have

bought a car of his own by now. I hope he gets a nosebleed
soon. An hour and a few minutes later a battered old sedan
comes retching up the road, going in the direction of town.
He has no choice, my old man. He gets in front of the
rattletrap and waves it to a stop. The driver pulls over
in the middle of the road, and he is, to my surprise, an
ordinary-looking middle-aged man.

'Delareyville?'

'What about Delareyville?'

'You're going there?'

'I don't know where I'm going, man. I've just put a new
piston and fixed the radiator of this shit. I'm just driving
around checking how far it will take me.'

'If it should allow you to keep going, will you go as far
as Delareyville?'

'Maybe. Look, I don't have a licence.'

'It's okay. I just want a lift. I won't rat on you.'

'Okay. Hop in. In the back, there's no seat here.'

'It's okay. Thank you.'

And my dad gets in the crate and says, 'See you soon, Prof,'
leaving me behind with people who are in all fairness still
strangers. There's a bit of sadness in me, but I promise
myself that I will be a good kid and leave my old man's
folks behind with very pleasant memories.

We go back to the house to find an early guest waiting
on the stoep with Grandpa. Grandpa hastens to introduce
us, the guy as Dirwe, just Dirwe, and me as Masimong's
Leungo.

'He came to see your father, all the way from Dikutung.
And where is that father of yours, eh? He's gone. That's

why I wanted him to stick around. Nobody's seen him, and he's already slunk out.'

The man Dirwe is family and apparently he comes to visit every now and then. He takes Diepeng by the hand and takes him to a tree behind the house. I follow them. Not that I want to. It's just that I can't sit here hanging out with the elders. There the guy orders Diepeng to take off his shirt. He obliges, my cousin Diepeng, removes the checked shirt from yesterday and goodness knows how many days before that, exposing a black round little stomach with a belly button like a bell. I've never seen one like that before.

'Is it sore, Diepeng?'
  'What?'
  'Sorry. Forget it.'

Dirwe speaks to me like he knows me, sends me for water, a bar of soap and Diepeng's washcloth in the house. When I come back with the things he's asked for he dips Diepeng's head in the water, wets the boy's shag of hair and rubs the bar of soap against it. He takes out a razor blade from his pocket and starts shaving Diepeng's head. I can't believe he's been keeping a razor blade in his pocket all this time, walking around with it. Like seriously. It looks painful the way the blade sweeps the hair off my cousin's head. But it doesn't look like he's feeling any pain. He's a tough little mister, sits still like one who's been around and experienced it all. The blade makes a wicked noise when it goes back and forth chipping off the hair. There's blood on his fingers but the guy won't stop. Thank goodness, a hundred times, my dad had the presence of mind to clean my head with that electrical shaving clipper before he brought me on this trip; otherwise I'd be in trouble. I'd most probably be the one next in line. I hope he's not about to turn on the assault on the twins. Now the little man starts to squirm. He's at it forever, the man called Dirwe, circling around the kid, punishing his scalp. When he is finished, which is like forty minutes later, he turns to me again and sends me to the house for washing powder. Diepeng himself tells me where I'll find it.

'In the kitchen. In a green margarine container. On top of the maize meal bin.'

The man dips the kid's head in the water again, blood and all, and sprinkles the nut with washing powder. Diepeng thrashes. He cannot be a man about this one. Dirwe won't be hurried. He takes his time washing his head, and when he's finished Diepeng's chiskop is the smoothest ever. But the man Dirwe is not done yet. He digs out a bottle from his pocket, and you won't believe what it contains. Brake fluid. It stings like a swarm of bees, the brake fluid that the man applies on the kid's bare scalp. The boy goes horse-wild. His face shrinks like a shoe. Now the man is done. He rinses the razor blade in the same water he used to wash Diepeng's head, and sits down to trim his moustache with the same blade. I've seen enough blood for one day.

I go back in the house to find Grandpa sitting alone in the lounge. Deep in thought. Wonder what one still thinks about when one has been alive for so long. If I was him I'd just sit around all day doing nothing. I join him, my grandfather, but I'm not sure if we will be able to make conversation with each other. He and I have never been alone before. This is history. Luckily he decides to be the one to start conversation between us. He asks me what it is like where we live and I tell him it's nice. He asks me how things are going on the school front and I tell him not too bad. He asks me what I want to be when I finish school and I tell him an auctioneer. He asks me what an auctioneer is and I explain a great deal and he doesn't understand. He doesn't understand why anybody would want to dedicate their lives to selling other people's stuff.

'You don't understand, Grandpa. It's not like that.'
     'Look, you're young. I know these things better.'

He asks me why I don't study towards becoming a minister instead, doesn't explain what kind of minister and I don't ask him. He asks me who I am and I tell him Leungo, son of Masimong and Sempheng Lerumo. He tells me my answer's vague and insufficient and I ask him to explain.

'You see, child, no one is just a name. Are you with me?'

He asks me to listen carefully to what he's about to tell me.

'Now listen to me, Leungo. Do you know what elders wake up to, every morning? We wake up to another bowl of tasteless soft porridge, and the probability we'll be dead very soon. You must never forget what I am about to tell you.'

He tells me I am a Motshweneng, that the totem of our clan is the monkey. The black monkey with a spiral tail. He tells me solidarity is our biggest strength. He says that we are nature's oldest geniuses, that we know the oldest secrets of time, of the earth and all its forests and caves. He tells me we feast on live scorpions like they were *mochana* (a kind of wild fruit), that we don't fear their sting. He tells me that we live forever, that no one that is one of us perishes if our gods can help it. He tells me that those who decide to straggle or wander off in a direction different from that of the whole group always find their way back. He tells me that like true simians we forget nothing but hold no grudges. He tells me our intelligence is intrinsic, that each one of us is born with it ingrained very deeply in the inner walls of the vessels that carry our very lifeblood. He tells me we have the sharp clairvoyance of creatures yet we're the most cultured of all human species. He tells me the only reason why we're not gods already is because we're still alive on earth. He tells me we don't cook herbs, that instead we pull them by the roots out of the earth and eat them raw and we don't even spit. He tells me the brightness of the stars multiplies when we shut our eyes and sleep. He says that mountains grow where they bury the healers and seers among us. He starts to get emotional, tears in his eyes and whatnot. He belches, dodders out of the living room to leave me munching on the great bone he has dumped on my lap.

Today is December the 31st, the last day of yet another calendar year. We haven't eaten any meat in the last two days. I don't find Grandma a sweet old woman anymore but a complaining, stingy one that I only get along with because she's family. She opens its door a crack, peeps into the fridge and says, 'Oh sunsets and sunrises, but what will we do?' and shakes her head and sends me out to the shop to buy canned fish, again. We've been eating canned fish and pap for the past two days. The last time we ate meat was when my father was here and Diepeng and I went and bought that sick chicken. I've been doing the chores alone, all of them, without any help from Diepeng, he upon whom praise was heaped by Grandma when she introduced him to me and my dad. 'Clever child, hard-working child; I would be older and much more bent if it weren't for him.' I'd secretly envied the bugger, told myself I'd go out of my way to score the same points with Grandma one day. Wishful thinking. I have been a donkey all forty-eight hours plus and Grandma has yet to show me any love. Grandpa I will leave out of things for now. I haven't spent much time with him. I avoid coming into his space these days because of the strange things he always says. I've spent the last two days frequenting that large supermarket with a silly name, most of the time on my own because Diepeng is often not around to go with me. It doesn't matter what time of the day it is, you always pass men old enough to be at home looking after their families in the streets, their shirts removed from their trunks and sticking out the back pockets of their jeans. They walk around in groups, stumbling, boozing in public. I wonder if they're also Batshweneng, if they belong to the same clan as Grandpa. If this is the kind of solidarity Grandpa spoke about in the little speech he gave me the other day then I'll pass thanks. I'll never be seen dead getting up to this kind of thing. I've also been buttonholed, in the two days that I have been frequenting the shops, by a mob of village youths that look more alike than they look different, some older than me, the majority younger. They went about making friendly conversation without really caring to establish who I was or introducing themselves. They heard me speak and were rendered amazed.

'*He banna. He monna, o* Mosotho?'

I answered no, told them I was a Motswana, a Motshweneng, the one that eats live scorpions for lunch, supper and breakfast. And they asked me:

'*Ao monna.* Then why do you say *fela* and not *hela*? Bachwening don't talk like that.'

And they'd walked away from me to return to whatever village pastime they were busy with before they came bothering me, tittering like bats. I'd get home and hand Grandma the tin of fish. Grandma would open the can immediately and take the fish out onto a flat plate and clean it of the small bones, missing a good number of them because her eyes are surely not as sharp as they used to be, and cook quickly and serve the food steaming hot. I've never finished a plate in the last two days. I'm hoping today we'll see something different. I'm hoping to see some meat. If I don't see meat on my plate today, or tonight, I swear I'm going on hunger strike. My dad didn't bring me here to suffer.

The day ages and there's no smell of meat; not in this house anyway. I've trespassed and forced its door open and looked into the fridge, and seen a lot of meat, in the freezer. Grandma for whatever reason keeps the fridge locked, but of course I'm no ninny. I can unlock it with a fingernail. Why she keeps the meat in there in the ice is beyond me. Diepeng seems to be the only one around here she knows she can trust. She gives him the key every now and then to check I don't know what's in there. Diepeng goes to the fridge, checks what he checks, turns the key again and takes the key back to Grandma. He never forgets to give it back. Grandma takes the key and lets it fall back in her seshweshwe frock. This is the third seshweshwe frock she's put on ever since I've been here, same cut, different colours. It is hotter than a mine down here but Grandma won't let us put water in the fridge to cool it for drinking.

'Cold water will make you sick.'
   'But, Grandma ...'
   'No. Don't be disrespectful.'

So we drink from an open-top bucket in the kitchen. Diepeng goes to the standpipe down the road every morning, gets in a line, waits his turn, fills up the bucket and lugs it back home. You can drink gallons of that water and your thirst will never be quenched. I wouldn't be surprised if it was proved that this water is the reason why Diepeng's tummy button has extended out from his stomach. Grandma's just being mean. I've been drinking cold water all my life and it has never once made me sick. I'd never live among these folks for two weeks. I wouldn't survive.

The meal at lunchtime is baked cakes and ginger beer. I don't know where the cakes came from because I have been home all day and Grandma has not once dipped her hands in the flour. I don't like ginger beer much, but as long as it keeps the mackerel at bay I am cool with it. It was just a matter of time before I started giving birth to tadpoles. I have never eaten so much fish in my life. The young ones, however, find ginger beer a little too hot on the palate. This is no liberation for them. They've had to contend with hot fish in the last two days, and now ginger beer. They pant helplessly. No one gives a toss what they're going through. This is how kids are raised in the bundus. They sweat, crinkle their faces and look all the uglier. I don't feel sorry for them no more. And why should I, when even their mother's child who's got the same blood as them doesn't give one shit about them? They open their mouths wide and fan their tongues with their hands. I want to burst out laughing but I do well to keep myself together. We finish our lunch and I get on top of the dishes. Luckily they're not smelly and oily today. I sprint through them. Apart from going out every now and then to draw water from the standpipe down the road Diepeng refuses to do anything these days. His scalp has freshly started acting up and now he's making it my problem. His scalp shone like a new spoon after that guy with smelly armpits razored him a couple of days ago. For a moment I even envied the chimp, actually. It was a clean job. No one saw this coming. His scalp is smooth as a spoon no more but covered in a white blanket of rash that one shouldn't look at if one wants to keep the food down. He was complaining of itchiness the whole day yesterday and I thought he was just being a sissy, but seeing him now I know he was being for real. I don't know why but I don't feel sorry for him. It's not like this rash is going to kill him or anything. Grandpa did tell me that no one that is one of us dies if the gods can help it, and I rather get a feeling the gods can do without a fourteen-year-old in their midst with a disgusting rash on his head and who refuses to do any work because of it.

It was quieter in the morning but now the atmosphere is heating up really quickly. Diepeng tells me there's a football match to take place at the local football ground, a match between the village's biggest rival clubs. He has snapped out of it. He's no longer a *bliksem* that sits around all day scratching his backside and telling us his head itches like he was carrying a sack of prickly pears on it. He fills a small bathtub with two jugs of cold water and starts bathing, in his bedroom. This is the first time he's had a bath since I've been here. I walk out. I don't like sticking around to watch when other people bath. Honestly. It's probably unbelievable, but it's true. Some people like it though. Diepeng himself sat in yesterday and watched me, and it was uncomfortable as hell scrubbing my backside and

118

scouring my eggs in front of him. Then he had the bottle to poke fun at me, call me a small boy and whatnot. And then he told me about the pubic hair that he says has started growing south of his inflated belly button. There are a few things I'm curious to see but pubic hair on a fourteen-year-old that is probably still only a few curly hairs that aren't even strong enough to absorb soap, is something I'd rather not see, so I leave him to it. I go to the living room and bundle myself on a sofa, wait until he's finished with the tub. I get the tub very soon. Five minutes is all this one needed. I'm not shocked. Nothing about this mister shocks me anymore. He hasn't bothered to, so I get a cloth and get busy scrubbing the bath of the mug's brown grime that has adhered to the plastic bathtub. It is only when the bath is looking almost spanking new again that I fill it up to the brim with warm water. I take to the boys' mother's room, my room for the time being, and scour myself clean.

I finish washing up and go outside to pour the soiled water into the growth behind the toilet. I find when I return to the house that Diepeng is waiting for me and is restless with excitement. He asks me to hurry up. I don't know where we're going, what he wants me to hurry up for.

'There's a match.'
   'There's a what?'
   'Ditlopo and Demolition are playing against each other.'
   'Dude, what are you talking about?'
   'Are you coming with me or not?'
   'Fine. Let's go.'

He takes out trotting. I am a bit undecided as to whether or not I should follow him. He's not stopping to give me another invitation but keeps going. I have no choice.

I can either go with him or stay here with Grandpa and Grandma. I get on my shanks and run after him. He turns to the left at the second turn and I do the same when I get there. His white rash skullcap shimmers in the sun with Grandma's ointment and he doesn't give a crab about it. Why must there always be a tragedy in the village involving a teenage boy that must be healed by the ointment of the oldest woman nearest to him? He turns to the right and I follow suit. He forks into the third compound on the right. I follow his lead. He vanishes in the crowd that fills this yard and leaves me behind, lost. No one cares to pay any attention, thankfully. Those whose eyes brush past me don't care to give me a second look. So I stand at the gate, alone, until one of the boys I've played with comes and sees me and comes over. 'Come,' says he to me. I follow him and we go past a thicket of bodies deeper into this vast compound.

The house at the heart of the yard is small and natty. There are two autos in here, a nice sedan that splutters some nice music from the open boot, and a van without a canopy. It really is a nice house this: yellow walls, a green tile roof, large windows and low green windowsills. There is no sign of Diepeng anywhere, so the boy and I chill together under one of the many trees in the vast yard. Until somebody blows a whistle and the masses start flocking into the house, and the dude gives me a sign and we follow the mob.

The house is not too bad inside either. As a matter of fact it gives my old grandpa's dull oldie a thorough walloping. There are people everywhere, grown-ass men who smell like rams. They sit on the floor, on the nice leather sofas, on the arms of the sofas, and others stand leaning against the walls. Somebody goes out to the sedan and turns down the music. There are so many people in here, but for some reason everyone is relaxed and it's all perfectly normal. We have not been in here for three minutes but it has started to get so stuffy it's nauseating. The music from the sedan has been killed so somebody takes to the floor to start addressing the mob. It is the young man on the picture on the wall with a pretty woman and a little baby. He's wearing sunglasses, in the living room. And ox-blood red formal shoes with a steel buckle. Formal pants, a brown leather belt and a black muscle vest. There's an air about him, an air of arrogance. He checks the guys out one by one.

'Gents, who's not here?' he asks.

'Standard, Leitlho and Mishaka, Coach.'

'No problem. It's only one of the fools on the starting line-up, and I'm taking him out.'

He has barely concluded his opening remarks when a couple of skinny, lanky guys come flying into the house. They are sweating. They pant like jackals. They have been running. They utter 'to whom it may concern' greetings, and then they greet the young man separately: '*Hola*, Coach,' they say. He doesn't greet them back. He's too busy throwing his weight around. This is a perfect opportunity for him to teach these two a lesson in front of everybody. He looks like the kind of guy who'd not think twice about exploiting this power that apparently he has. Sure enough, that's what he does. He takes a minute to respond, then he looks them straight in the eyes like he was their lover and was mad at them after finding them getting up to no good. They squirm like reptiles in the frying pan. He indicates with a movement of his head that he wants them to go outside the house. They oblige. He walks out behind them, walks them out. Outside he makes them do push-ups, right there in front of the house, and he comes back in to get on with it. Some of these men are older than him yet his very presence makes them fidget like kids. Back inside he tells his men that winning has never been as important as it is going to be today. He implores the defenders to be hard with their tackles. He tells the two centre backs that there is one guy in particular that they will have to be hard and intelligent when they deal with, the opposition's number fifteen. He tells the wingers to push to the line and whip in high balls for the target man. He says they must also come back and assist defensively, especially if they should score first. He tells the midfielders to be as hard in dealing with the opposition as the defenders. He tells them to take long-range shots and to push and to keep the ball as close as possible to the opposition's eighteen yards and win as many set pieces as possible. For whoever will start upfront he has only one thing to say: do not be caught offside. The last statement disappoints me. He's been talking so well, so intelligently. How can he expect a striker to not be caught offside? What does it matter if a striker's caught offside a hundred times? Why if he doesn't have anything better to say can't he at least ask the striker to head the balls down that the wingers are going to whip in for the midfielders to take shots at goal? He continues blabbering and I am not interested anymore. The two lanky guys have done all one hundred push-ups as they were told to do and they have come doddering back into the house like ghosts, exhausted. He sees them coming back in but does not bother to say another word to either of them. They don't know it, but he's already told all of us that he's benching their backsides.

The time comes and he starts calling out the names of those who made the starting eleven. He mentioned earlier that he will be trying the 4–5–1 formation for the first time. He calls out ten names including the goalkeeper's. He takes his time deciding who is going to be the sole target man upfront. He paces back and forth. The house is quiet as a grave. A lady comes clopping into the living room amidst the silence, from the bedrooms. I notice at once that she's the pretty lady in the framed photograph dangling on a nail on the wall. She's not as pretty in real life as she is in that picture. She carries a human being in her arms, a creature that is neither a fully fledged young child nor a baby. He must be two and a half going on three, that kid in the woman of the house's arms. The woman leans against the wall and slowly starts pulling down the neckline of her shirt, in the passage where the living room stops and the rest of the house begins. The garment obliges, spills out a limp brown breast that the toddler in arms pounces on immediately. The little old man takes the crooked nipple between his teeth that must be sharper than mine and my whole body cringes. What if he bites her? He's not at it for very long, the nursling with ears like trumpets. He's had a skinful, and he leaves the organ hanging, green veins and all. The woman leaves the organ outside her blouse, in case the little mister discovers his thirst is not quite fully quenched and goes again. It is an ugly breast, uglier than most I've seen. It is not smooth and round but wrinkled and flat. The circles are darker, and bigger. It's a very sorry sight. It's got a bit of stretch marks too, this boob. I have never seen stretch marks on a boob in all my life. If I was that kid I would never suck on that one. I would rather starve. She tries again some five minutes later to dunk it in his mouth but the boy won't have it. That means he is full, for now. She yanks her blouse and the veined organ falls back in its cradle. She puts the little man down and he streaks off out to his daddy. That one with formal shoes and a muscle vest has decided who the striker is going to be. He calls out the last name to complete the starting eleven.

'Hey, Pat?'

All eyes fall on the guy Pat, and he's beaming.

'Yes, Coach?'
    'Won't you be a brother and do something for the team?'
    'Anything, Coach. What does Coach want me to do?'
    'I like that. Thanks. Lend Kotsi your boots, will you? Kotsi, you're starting up front. Remember what I said earlier, okay? Whatever you do don't be caught offside. Come on, boys, get in the gear.'

The guy Pat shakes his head incredulously. He's peeved, pissed. He lends Kotsi more than just the boots. He gives him the whole bag, bandages, shin pads and all. The guys start to strip and don't care one bit that there's a woman and children in the audience. They all look alike when they're half naked. They're skinny and tall and black as chocolate, and they've got alligators snoozing in the holding sections of their threadbare underpants. The guys sing loud songs as they dress up in a green-and-white kit. The goalkeeper dresses up in a colourful shirt and a black pair of long tracksuit pants. The team crowds up in the back of the van parked outside without a canopy and the van moves. I join Diepeng and the other small boys and we trot behind the van to the football ground that is only a block away from the beautiful clubhouse.

'So what is the name of this team, boys?'

'Demolition. I told you.'

'No, you didn't. You just told me the names of both teams.'

'That's what I just said. If I told you the names of both teams it means I told you the name of this one.'

'Whatever, dude.'

We arrive at the ground to find a maroon-and-black-dressed army already on the battlefield, waiting for us. The turnout of spectators is mad. I've never seen anything like this back in Tlhabane. There is such a buzz in the atmosphere I struggle to believe that I am still in this dull village where I have been an unhappy, bored prisoner for the previous week or so. I search the field for the opposition's player with the number fifteen on his shirt. I locate him. He's short and plump and has an ugly mop of dreadlocks on his head. I look at the man and I cannot even guess what that coach had in mind when he singled him out as the dangerman. The referee, a young man dressed in his own street clothes, takes the money from both captains, counts it and pockets it, sets his watch and blows the match underway. The game runs for ten minutes before the opposition fires home. The boys and I are standing behind the goals of our team. The game runs on. The whistle blows for half-time with the scoreline still reading one–nil to the opposition. The teams converge on either half of the pitch. The coach is fuming. He fits like a prophet. He cusses like a barbarian. He's mad at everybody. 'Dammit man,' he yells at Kotsi. 'I spent the whole afternoon telling you not to be caught offside and you went and got caught offside how many times? Huh? Fifteen times? Twenty? You get caught offside once in the second half and I'm pulling you out.' He splutters a long, heated speech and doesn't go easy on them until the referee blows for the teams to get up and get back on the bare park for the second half to get underway. Everyone except the players leaves the field. We follow our keeper, me and my two companions, to the goals on the other side. The game is on again, and soon an accident happens, a horrible accident. The coach singled out number fifteen as the dangerman but I'm not sure he had this in mind when he did. I'm not sure he saw it coming, for Diepeng my cousin sure as hell didn't. The goalkeeper of the opposition throws a long ball forward and it falls on the feet of a midfielder who flicks it on by way of a neat little back-heel. The ball spins quickly towards the byline. Our dangerman pursues it. It rolls away quickly and he has to streak like mad if he hopes to catch it before it goes out for a goal kick. The ball is on the line when the man gets to it. He tries to cut it goalwards with the toe of his right foot and he misses the ball completely. Now he's out of balance and in full speed. It all happens too fast. He comes flying out of the pitch and crashes into my poor defenceless cousin Diepeng who stands next to another boy on that side of the goals. His shoulder strikes young Diepeng on the face and trundles him into involuntary flight. The boy teeters off with feet barely touching the ground and is stopped by a shrubby xerophyte a hundred metres out. 'Check that kid,' somebody says, and the game continues like nothing has happened. I can't believe they're carrying on with the game. 'Solidarity is our strength,' echoes my grandpa's words again in my ears. I don't know if it has anything to do with solidarity what I now do, but I take off running to the thorny tree that has taken Diepeng prostrate prisoner. He's out of it. He's not even thrashing. He lies there on his back, motionless. The tree's thorns drink gladly from the flesh of my cousin. I'm about to brave it and go in when a grown-up man comes to my rescue. He braves the stinging thorns and goes in to pluck Diepeng off. He carries him like a corpse and places him prone on the ground. I turn my cousin over and make him lie on his back. He's bleeding badly. He's bleeding, quite badly. He's hurt.

'Don't make him lie on his back, you moron. Can't you see his nose is bleeding?'

And somebody rolls him over again. What does it help? The man who helped me get my cousin out of that tree walks away from the patient, and I'm left on my own to do something. I don't know what to do. 'Diepeng? Dips? Can you hear me? Diepeng?' Nothing. I take off my beloved double mercerised blue shirt, bend to the ground and start tapping my hand against Diepeng's face in an attempt to staunch the flow of blood. It seems to work. The flow stops eventually. That was one wicked blow that took him out, but this one is a fighter. It takes a few minutes, but slowly he starts to open his eyes and return to consciousness. He sits up on his backside, with some effort, and starts to spit out red lumps of goodness knows what. I hope he's not spitting out any of his innards. The football is in full flight still, and they've all forgotten about the poor kid who took a knock to his face and hit the ground in a heap. Diepeng's lips are torn and tattered and hang loosely like strips of meat hung to dry into biltong. I pull him up to his legs and help him home with his arm around my neck for support. I explain to Grandma what happened and she takes over. I wash my hands, put on a fresh shirt and slink out back to the football ground. My friend is still here, the same one I chilled with earlier at the clubhouse, tells me our guys have equalised. I tell him it's dangerous that we should continue standing here behind the goals and he agrees with me. We move away and go and stand as far away from the goals

as possible. Our guys score goal number two with a few
seconds left on the clock and the referee blows the full-time
whistle. The van takes the victorious soldiers back to the
clubhouse and we don't run behind it like we did when we
came to the ground. Another fellow, a friend of the guy
I'm with, joins us. We trot slowly behind the masses, me
and the two fellows. It is three of us until three girls come
trotting past us and one of my two companions calls out
at them.

'*He nyena, emang hao.*'

They stop. We're almost upon them and they take off
running. They're all three more or less the same age as us.
They stop again, and run off again. It becomes a game. The
guys, my friends, get in the mood. They increase their pace.
I'm not participating in this one. I lag behind, deliberately.
They won't have any of it. They make me take part against
my will.

'*Tlo tlhe monna. Khobakhoba ntja. A re ba lelekise.*'

Come on, dog, trot along. Let's chase after them. That is the
request, plain and without crooks but pretty intimidating
for someone like me. I'm lost, bogged down in a wide pan
of confusion. We take a direction taken by the girls and
that drives us away from where everyone else is going,
which is in all fairness where we should all be going, back
to the clubhouse. When we left the football ground we
set out to go back to the clubhouse with the team, but
now we're running off into the parts of the village I have
never seen, chasing after this trio of girls to do with them
I don't know what when we catch them. I feel deceived,
like that guy when the coach made him lend that other guy

his boots when he almost knew that that position was his. The guys run fast and I have little choice but to step it up. We gain on the girls. Something that I don't like happens. The guys without a word and with some careless village cunning pick out the two pretty girls and frolic with them and tickle them. I don't do anything, not until somebody tells me what's going on. The tickled girls chuckle like dolls and run off again. I realise now what's going on and I want to turn and go back to my grandparents' house. I can't be out here getting up to monkeyshines like this when I've got a hurt cousin back home to go check on. I have seen that girl close up who's supposed to be my playmate and I'm pretty sure I'm not interested. The village guys, however, are too excited to note my discomfort. They streak off again in pursuit of their chosen girls. I run along, just not with the same pace. I am playing my own game, seeing to it always that I fall behind long enough to arrive too late. The stupid game goes on and on and no one tires of it. I've never seen and participated in anything quite this stupid in my life. I make it appear as if I'm struggling with a pain in the leg, keep getting there too late. This girl is seriously ugly.

'What's wrong, man? Heh? Townboy, what is it? Are you afraid of girls?'

Peer pressure has been the topic of the few discussions and debates I've ever taken part in at school and that of a few essays I have ever written, and for the first time in my life I fall helpless prey to it. I move in on the girl and I start tickling her, with more fingers than heart really. Her flesh is tough as a boy's. She looks at me and looks like she wants to punish me for neglecting her the last three stops or so when the other boys gave their girls some attention. She plonks an open hand on my privates and the onlooking quartet bursts out laughing. She pulls me by the neck and kisses me. She's harassing me right now. She's all over me like a pickpocket and I can't even turn and run. I'm a little dumbstruck to be honest. The whole thing is very unreal. She puts her hand over her clothes on her pubes and asks me: 'You want to touch?' I don't want to touch her there and I say no thanks and the quartet neighs out again.

'What's your name?'
    'My name? Leungo.'
    'Okay. It's nice. Don't you want to know what mine is?'
    'Tell me.'
    'Kedigoletse.'
    'What does it mean?'
    'How should I know? Go ask my dad.'

We sit on the ground in a circle and they make me tell them about my life and about Tlhabane. I speak of my township with a love I never knew I possessed. They ask me if I have a girlfriend back home and I want to say yes and tell them her name is Lesego, but I can't lie. For one thing lying is not a part of my nature. I can't lie and not feel bad. And then I can't lie about Lesego. Yes, I wish I was older and had enough balls to walk up to her and spew into her ears the truth about the goings-on in my heart, but at this stage she is only my girl friend. I swallow my pride and tell them no, I don't have a girlfriend. They ask me if I've ever done it and I tell them no again, tell them I'm still too young to even think about it. They tell me all that is about to change. Somebody comes up with a suggestion to which everybody but me bleats a savage baa of agreement. I'm outnumbered. It's on. We're having group sex tomorrow. Sex in a group. One room, all six of us. Windows closed.

Curtains drawn. Partner to partner. They know just the place. It's safe. No one will see us. It will be a lot of fun. They can't wait. The ugly girl tells me I'm in for a lot of fun, tells me none of the other two girls can do the things she can do.

'Please. Like you've done it before.'
   'I was not talking to you, Mamiki.'

I want to melt into the sand. We split. The girls go that way and we go the other way. The fellows accompany me home. They want me to tell them more about Rustenburg, the city, but I can't talk anymore. I'm still in shock. My head spins. My ears ululate like a toothless woman that has had a little too much to drink. Sex? Geez.

It has darkened up quite significantly by the time I get back home. Grandma's fuming. She's been waiting at the door, ready to tear into me.

'How could you abandon him when he needed you? Hmm? Leungo, what kind of cousin are you? Is it that you don't have siblings the thing that makes you so inconsiderate? Are you always like this? Heh? Answer me.'

I think it's all very unfair but I don't tell Grandma that much. I keep quiet. If only she knew how dearly I had treasured that shirt of mine and had seen how I had not even stopped to think twice before I took it off and started using it to staunch my cousin's blood she would not be coming down this hard on me. Diepeng is fast asleep. Grandma tells me she's made him take two pain pills and one and a half sleeping pills. She pulls the blankets off Diepeng's face and a horror greets my eyes. His face is swollen all over. I feel guilty that I left him, but what would I have done? Maybe Grandma's right. I could have stuck around, and I should have. But my sticking around will not have prevented the swelling. It is a rough December for this poor chap, it really is. I'm just glad I've had nothing to do with any of his bad luck. There's no reason for me to feel guilty about anything. Grandma's just being unfair. Grandma tells me in no uncertain terms that I am not to leave the house tomorrow and the rest of the days that I am still to spend here unless she herself sends me out to the supermarket. Unbelievable. It is a rough end to the year for me too, when one looks at it real close. I go to the kitchen to find pap and spinach waiting for me in the pots and a whole pile of dirty dishes waiting to be washed. This is the first time I will go to bed without having touched meat on December the 31st. When will I escape from this place? I can't wait for the eighth, I really can't. I've had enough of this village. I know it doesn't sound right but I've had enough of Grandma too. I'm tired. It's been a long day. I put the pots together, take off the lids and start digging in. Grandma catches me in the act and tears some more into me.

'Stop it, child, stop it. Why do you eat from the pot like a drunk when there are so many plates in this house? Huh? Stop it at once. You'll get *sechwabu* and die with your spine crooked like the rainbow. What does that mother of yours teach you?'

I take it personal. I'd actually prefer that my mom be kept out of this. I don't tell Grandma such because I respect her, but I don't like the way she attacks my mom. She probably doesn't even know her. I don't think my mom has ever come down here. I dish what's left of the chow into an enamel plate and bury all of it in four takes. I speed through the dishes, brush my teeth and go straight to bed.

The heat tonight is worse than all the heat we've had in the last couple of days. I peel down to my underpants and splay myself over Diepeng's *phate*. Due to the extent of his injuries Grandma has decided that Dips needs to sleep on his mother's bed, alone, so he has freedom to move and sleep right in the centre of the double bed.

'That way there's no chance he'll fall off,' she told me earlier.

'There was no chance he'd fall off his *phate*, Grandma.'

'What was that?'

'Nothing. I just wanted to know where I will be sleeping. Where am I supposed to sleep, Grandma?'

'Oh. You're sleeping with the twins in the other room.'

It's not right. It's all very upsetting how I am being treated so unfairly. There was nothing else I can do so I did exactly as I was told. I washed the dishes and came straight here, to Diepeng's room that he shares with his siblings. Here I am, flat on the floor on a *phate*, for the first time ever. This thing offers me no comfort whatsoever. It doesn't help much that Diepeng's blankets leak a smell I can't stomach. I try to pull one over my head and I can't. I fail to endure. How am I supposed to fall asleep now, when I always sleep with a blanket over my head? I'm not being funny. These blankets stink. Not even men that I've seen on television that are said to be champs of extreme sport could handle them. The twins are out cold like stones. I pray that I fall asleep before they start breaking wind and snoring and grinding teeth. Just when I thought sharing a bedroom with my uncle and his wife was the worst thing that could ever have happened to me.

Two hours in, and here I am still. There's no chance I will be falling asleep any time soon. Tonight is New Year's Eve, the busiest, most eventful day anywhere on earth, and here I am shrouded in stuffy blankets in a stuffy room with tots who snore like the elderly. I remember my habitat Tlhabane and what we got up to last December, my friends and I. We didn't turn in at seven. In the normal world out there nobody goes to bed at seven on a day like this. We lit long crackers and set the atmospheres ablaze with colours. We sang jolly songs. We danced. We ran up and down the streets without fear of getting lost or running into trouble. We welcomed the new year with a great collective thrill. Look at me now. There's not a sound out there in the dark. Everyone has crawled in. I won't be here this time next year. I swear. My dad will have to inject me with methylated spirits before he bamboozles me into packing a bag.

I turn and toss, and toss and turn. Nothing doing. It is when you cannot fall asleep that you start thinking too much. The same happens to me. My mind starts wandering. What an eventful day this one has been. I trace the day back to the yellow-and-green clubhouse. I remember the build-up to the football match. That floppy boob shows itself again and I avert my mind's eye quickly. I recall the football match, great event until the damned accident. I recall the last event of the day and remember again with disgust that I didn't like it very much. I remember again the pact they had, sitting in a circle like King Arthur and his cabinet. Sex? I squirm. I shudder. Legofi and I are the tightest friends in the world and we chat about everything: cars, football, music, movies, even girls. But sex? We never even touch on the subject. We've never once touched on it. What do children know about sex? How do they do it, anyway? Surely they push flat chests into one another.

And then what? Does the boy grope with a clueless finger for a socket into which his excited jewel must be slotted or does he know automatically when he's there which way to go? What does it feel like when the probing rocket has made it beyond the toll gate and rattles quietly through the burning coals? Do a hundred darts of mad excitement find the heart and render one insane? Does one sweat as much as Mokuru did in that narration told by Maitirelo Malehonyane the other day? Can children handle all that madness and sweat and pressure, and pleasure if indeed that is also to be attained? Could I do it? If I should take the mad village children up on their challenge tomorrow and go and get myself dirty with them, will I do it well enough and not make a monkey of myself? What a mess. Why did I not fake madness and get institutionalised before my old man brought me to this mad village? Why does the next sun not refuse to rise? Being here with these guys in this stuffy atmosphere in this bedroom is a lot of torture, but surely it is a hundred times better than sex, and not just sex but sex with that girl. I don't even have pubic hair. How can those rascals expect me to know how to do that nasty thing? Gross kids. That's what they are. Disgusting, twisted children. Legofi's going to think I'm making up half the things I'm going to tell him when I go back home.

The first of January. The break of dawn. The break of the new year.

'Good morning, Grandpa. Happy new year.'

'You're talking to me, child?'

'Yes, Grandpa.'

'Don't be stupid, Leungo. I thought you were bright, son. There's no such thing as a new year.'

135

'But Grandpa ...'

'Look, forget about it.'

Grandma has been up for a while, cleaning the house, coddling over her favourite grandson, applying all kinds of ointments to his wounds. She's been waiting for me for a long time to get up, and here I am now, on my feet and out of the covers. She sends me out to the shops for tea bags and a packet of macaroni. Diepeng's up and about when I come back. I almost don't recognise him. The rash on his scalp is whiter than ever. And his face, shame. The poor chap looks like he was in a duel with a horse. Grandma sends me back to the supermarket for *mageu*, tells me she has been trying to feed him soft porridge but he cannot get his mouth open, not wide enough for a teaspoon to pass through. She says I must ask for a straw. I return from the supermarket and I have forgotten the straw and Grandma hurls heavy words at me and sends me back for it. She tells me when I return that I am to look after Diepeng until he recovers and reminds me again that I am not to leave the house the whole day. She tells me that if that tragedy had happened to me Diepeng would never have left my side once. I don't know what to say. All I know is that this is going to be the dullest New Year's Day ever.

'Are we going to eat some meat today, Grandma?' I ask her.

'No, child. You see, it was my plan to cook some beef stew today. But Diepeng can't even open his mouth to take in a spoon of porridge. We can't eat meat while he suffers.'

'But, Grandma, he's got his *mageu*. He'll eat meat when he recovers. He will recover, very soon.'

'Stop it, Leungo. I don't like how you only think of yourself. Where have you ever seen meat and macaroni going into the same plate anyway?'

I give up. Grandma lights the paraffin stove, mounts the pot full to the lid with potatoes, macaroni tubes, and water. I don't think she likes me much to be honest. She's punishing me for something, and I don't even know what it is. I don't deserve it. I'm just a kid. She turns off the stove, lines up the enamel plates and dishes up. Diepeng can't open his jaws wide enough for macaroni either. Grandma's close to tears. I feel nothing. Nothing for Grandma and nothing for the disfigured guy. We'd be munching on some meat now, if the little shit had the presence of mind to duck out of the way when that mug came teetering his way. If this guy had half a brain he'd still be an idiot. I can't believe I'm even related to him. One of these days I'm going to ask him to show me his books. I bet there's not one six out of ten in there. Canned fish is nothing; I've never liked macaroni. Macaroni tastes like vomits. I don't think Grandma's even put salt in this macaroni. If you put soil in a bowl and mixed it with water it would turn out ten times tastier than this food. I am so angry I have to grit my teeth to stop myself from crying. It should actually be Diepeng's turn to do the dishes but I don't even want to start that one. I do what I have to do, grab all the dishes and take them to the kitchen to wash them. I hope my mom never finds out I was a kitchen girl around here or she'll get ideas. I miss her, my mother. I miss her like nothing in the world.

It is late in the afternoon when whistles sound at my grandfather's gate. I peep out the window and you won't believe who's standing out there. It is the rascals I hung out with yesterday. Dammit. I'd forgotten about the stupid sex thing planned for today. I ask one of the twins, and I still can't tell them apart, to go to the gate and ask them who they're looking for, and if they say they're looking for me to tell them that I am not around. The bugger botches the job. He opens his mouth and shits with it.

'Are you looking for Leungo?'
  'How do you know?'
  'Leungo's not around. Go.'
  'You're lying. We saw him. He's in the house.'
  'You saw him?'
  'Yes.'
  'Are you his friends?'
  'Just go call him, okay?'

He darts back in the house and tells me my friends are looking for me. Dumb child. I remember for the first time that I'm actually grounded, and what a relief it is too. It's not the worst punishment in the world after all. Now I can show my face. I walk out the front door all the way to the gate and tell the idiots myself that I can't leave, that Grandma has grounded me because I must look after Diepeng. They try to persuade me to disobey Grandma and I refuse. I refuse to be a victim of peer pressure for the second day in a row. They resort to vulgar language. In an attempt to mock me one of them tells the other out loud that I don't have a penis and I'm afraid they're going to find out and laugh at me. I stand my ground. They hurl yet more swear words at me and I remain standing. '*O ntoto ya mosimanyana hela wena sani*,' they say, and get on their way. They're not bad guys. It's just that I don't dig that sex thing very much. What happened to children being children?

Another day. Four days it has been since the unmannered buggers came looking for me. Three days to go now, only three days left before I get out of here. Actually, it's only two days left because I'm leaving on the third one. Yes. Today's the fifth; I'm leaving on the eighth. The observation injects excitement into my system, excitement and hope. Diepeng's face is clearing up. His hair is also growing again, and the rash vanishing. The food rack is parched; the fridge only has a tomato, a carton of *mageu* and a carton of fresh milk. Grandma does not even keep it locked anymore.

'What happened to the meat that was in there, Diepeng?'
    'What meat?'
    'The red meat that was in the freezer, a few days ago?'
    'Oh? That meat? It was not our meat.'
    'Whose meat was it?'
    '*He monna*, my body's sore all over. I know nothing about the meat you're talking about. Go ask Grandma.'

We eat pap everyday, pap and a powder that turns into scrambled eggs, believe it or not, when it gets mixed with water. Pap and spinach. Pap and milk. From six o'clock in the morning until six o'clock at night, everyday. The weather's too hot. I am starting to get pimply. I still sleep in Diepeng's room with the twins, and the smell of his blankets has not killed me yet. Grandma says the electricity coupon is running out and forbids us from watching TV during the day anymore. I don't know what to do with myself. I take a *phate* and go to lie next to Grandpa under the tree behind the house. He's not asleep. He asks to take a look at my member. '*Mpontsha nyonywane ya gago mosimane,*' he says. He's not joking, you know. I turn to look him in the eye and find he is dead serious. He really wants to have a look at my willy. Just when I thought I was safe from lunatics, in here and not out there with the crazy kids of this village. I do as he says and wrench out the millipede.

He cranes forwards, bends in his chair over me and takes my penis in his bare hands. He turns it this way and the other way, inspecting it. He shakes his head.

'Just as I thought. Don't worry, I blame your father.'

This whole thing is uncomfortable. I'm too pissed to ask him what he's going on about. He tells me I'm old enough, that it's time for me to be taken to the mountain. He tells me that all boys my age are circumcised and have had their rites. Now I get nervous, like seriously frightened. I don't know what this old man is planning but I don't like it. I wish I never came out here to be alone with him. I wish I was in a taxi back home already. My willy's back in my underpants and my zippers zipped tight. I pee myself a little, and who wouldn't? 'Next winter you must come,' he tells me. My heart falls back into its holster. Relief. I'm not coming back to this place of horrors, not ever. In your dreams, Grandpa. In your dreams. Circumcision? The mountain? I would never. Who knows, maybe it was the same thing my dad fled. I can't hang out with this guy anymore. There's something not right about Grandpa, seriously. I leave him alone under the tree and take to the boys' room for an early night.

The next days blooms and screams by like a wheelbarrow. Late in the afternoon my grandmother does something she hasn't done in a couple of days. She sends me out to the supermarket. I have a few coins in my bag. I count them. Five rands and forty-five cents. I get to the supermarket and my first stop is the payphone outside. I dial my aunt Sebeto's number and ask to speak to my mother. Aunt Sebeto tells me she's not at my place, that she and Malome Jobe have found a room a few blocks away from my home and have moved out. My heart bleeds. I say goodbye. I tell her I love her and she tells me she loves me too. I ask her to greet Malome Jobe and I hang up. I check the remaining balance and there's still enough for another call. Three rands twenty-five cents is what's left. I dial Dimpaletse Prince's wife's number. It rings. Luck is on my side. Dimpaletse Prince himself answers and he is at my place with my dad and the guys. He hands the device to the old man whose genes sculptured me. His voice is sweeter than I have ever heard it. I remember now that yesterday was my birthday. He reminds me. But he's also missed it. He says happy birthday to me today but my birthday was actually yesterday. I can't believe I forgot such an important day. I have conquered a decade. I ask my dad about Mom and he tells me she's doing fine but throwing up a lot. I ask him if she's well and he laughs. He says she is but tells me I shouldn't be surprised when I get back home and find her still sick and throwing up, that he thinks it might go on for a while.

'I can't believe you're laughing about it, Dad. It could be serious.'

'She'll be alright, Prof. Trust me.'

I ask him how he knows she'll be alright and he tells me he just knows. He's in great mood and it rubs off on me. Tears fill my sinuses. I ask him about the guys and he tells me they're broke as jackals but otherwise they're fine. He tells me they're going to brew their own malt tomorrow, that times are tough. He says that he and the other guys ate brown bread yesterday, without butter or margarine, and drank beer for lubrication. He says old Seolo Magang couldn't eat, that he had a painful mouth. He says Seolo Magang went to the local clinic and they told him he must see a doctor. He says Seolo Magang didn't have enough money so they all donated what they could and when there was enough in the kitty Benedict took him to a doctor. He doesn't quite know as yet what the story is with the old man's mouth but tells me the doctor's note is still at our place, that old Seolo Magang might have forgotten it there or left it on purpose. He tells me there's a funny word in the card written in bold letters and he spells it out for me. P-Y-O-R-R-H-O-E-A. He asks me if I know what the word means and the phone dies before I can provide him with an answer. I was going to tell him I didn't know and he'd have said, 'Don't worry Prof, you'll know one day'. This has actually been the first ever telephone conversation between myself and my dad, ever. I've never had to phone him once in my life. He's always been there. Wonder if he would have told me he loved me, at the end of the conversation if the coupon had lasted out for three more minutes. Well, if he'd ventured to tell me he loved me I would have told him I loved him too. And I miss him. And I think he's the coolest dad in the world. My spirits carried aloft by my father's liveliness, I walk away from the payphone into the supermarket, buy onions and go back to that house. Nothing new happens tonight. Grandma cooks and dishes up, we eat our supper and everybody goes to bed when I go to the kitchen to do the dishes. We go to sleep. I sleep before the twins who are in the grandparents' bedroom taking turns massaging Grandma's legs with their little hands. I don't take my pants off for fear the little rascals may come in while I'm fast asleep and get an idea to peep into my briefs. Not that they've done it before, you know.

The village cocks announce the arrival of another day. I wake up early. Only today to go. My spirits are bright, and why not? I'm all over the place. I help Grandma clean the house. I go to the public standpipe and draw a full bucket of drinking, ten litres of it. Grandma sends me to the supermarket for battery cells and I drag the twins along. I've never wanted to be seen with them but today I'm doing things differently. Big mistake too. I get the battery cells and pay for them, but when it's time to go back home the boys are nowhere to be seen. I last saw them when I went into the supermarket and they stayed outside. They probably know the way back home, I'm sure they do, so I don't bother looking for them. I have turned only one corner when they come running after me. They stop running when they reach me. They're panting. They've each got a tin of condensed milk. They volunteer to tell me how they got the tins before I ask them.

'Malome Dirwe bought them for us.'

'Don't lie to me. I didn't see Dirwe at that shop. He wasn't there.'

'Not that one. The other one.'

'Which other one?'

'You don't know him.'

And they've already opened holes in the tins and they're busy sucking the sap out of them. They've pinched the tins of condensed milk, the little fuckers, because the guard from the supermarket comes and pounces on us from the back. He grabs me by the scruff of the neck, like I know what's going on.

'What are you doing?'

'You stole from the shop. You're coming with me.'

'Don't be crazy, man. You saw me at the till. I paid for these batteries.'

'I'm not talking about the batteries. I'm talking about

the condensed milk that your friends stole.'

'They stole the condensed milk?'

'Don't act stupid. Of course they did, and you know it. It was probably your great idea.'

'What? You don't even know me.'

'Exactly.'

He takes all three of us back to the shop, pulling us by the clothes like we were a bunch of common lowlifes. I try to reason with him, explain what happened, but he's not interested. He's too busy being a super cop, the one who gets the bad guys and shames them in full view of the world. I have been coming alone to this shop for the last three days and I have not had one problem. Can't believe these kids dragged me into this mess. I hate scandals. I don't even have money to buy my way out of the crap. The man has taken us right through the supermarket into the storeroom. The manager of the place is not interested in long stories and explanations. He's all for punishment. He makes me bend over and whips my backside. He gives me about five lashes, all on exactly the same spot. The only punishment the ugly shits get is the tins of condensed milk taken from them and thrown in the rubbish pit. They release us soon as the last whip has stung my backside. I want to tell the lot of them a piece of my mind but I'm wise enough to keep the reins on. They'll probably just be petty and whip me some more. I wait until we've turned the first corner before I start taking my revenge on the little dogs. I run behind them kicking their asses non-stop until we're back at the house. I have no mercy for thieving shits. I don't stop kicking them until they're right at the door. Grandma wants to know if I am mad and I tell her yes and I tell her exactly what happened that brought on the madness. She throws her elbows on her head. She splutters

a thousand exclamations. She doesn't believe it, throws her
hands in the air. She blames me. She says I've embarrassed
the family, shamed it. She tells me the boys have been living
here all their lives and they have never once pinched a grain
of salt. She tells me to my face that I'm a bad influence, a
kid from a bad family. She tells me she thinks I'd better
leave, today already, before I do more damage to the boys'
heads. I can't believe it. She pulls a handkerchief out of her
clothes, unties the knot and takes out two blue notes that
she has been keeping in there for nearly two weeks.

'Take. This is your transport money that your father
Masimong left with me. You're leaving, today.'

I take the notes. The message is clear. She wants me gone.
I have already washed up. I pull my suitcase out from my
aunt Salang's wardrobe, stuff my belongings in it without
caring to pack them nicely, put my cap on and set the peak
to the side where I know the sun will be burning, and
utter quick goodbyes. Grandpa says I must honour our
agreement and return in winter for that thing we talked
about and I say nothing. I won't be in a hurry to come
back here, that's for sure. Grandma pouts her lips and
murmurs something. I don't hear what she says and with
all due respect I don't make an attempt to hear. Nobody
accompanies me to the main road where I will board a
taxi, not even Diepeng who I carried from the football
ground with blood spraying like rain from his torn veins.
The twins stick their heads out the door when I get to the
gate but I am not interested. I don't wanna see them again
in a long time. I want to show them my middle finger. They
better mend their ways or they'll wind up in jail one day.
An hour later and I'm in the town of Delareyville. It was
two hundred rand that money Grandma gave me in that

incensed fit. I am only going to need some sixty-five rands to go from this point to Tlhabane. That calculation leaves me with a lot of free money in my pockets. There's some distance to go from here to Rustenburg so I better fill up with some real chow. Been a while since I last tasted decent food anyway. I find my way back to that restaurant no problem. I order a plate of rice and chicken and grab a seat, wait for some ten minutes before they call me back to the counter to fetch my chow. I don't take my time but rush through it, this late breakfast or early lunch or whatever this meal is. My stomach is chuffed. Real food at last. I pick my way out of the restaurant out to the taxi rank. Today's my lucky day. I didn't wait half as long as my dad to get a taxi from that village to here, and I get in the taxi to take us to Rustenburg and it doesn't take forever to get full. The sliding door's slammed shut and the khombi hits the highway. I'm going back home, dig it?

The trip back is anything but uneventful. As a matter of fact it is more eventful than the trip here, a week and a couple of days ago. One of the passengers that we ride with back to Rustenburg is some trumpet. He takes a while to get started, but once he gets out of the blocks there is no stopping him. He is a tall man and he cannot sit with his shoulders up and his neck straight, so he balances his arms on the top edge of our seat and his head hovers above the head of the dumpy dude next to me, all the way back. The dumpy guy's eyes are weary and red and barely holding up, and he looks like he's been to the end of the world and back in the last few hours or so. He yawns wide like a hippo every five hundred metres or so. He really is wiped out. The poor man is not digging the fact that the giant's chin hangs over his crown like this, but what can he do? No one in his right mind picks a fight with heavyweights like this, especially not shorties like himself. So he sits smouldering and endures it, the middle-aged man. It doesn't help him much that the hulk can't stop yapping. At first he tries to avoid it by leaning forward, but finds he is too tired to keep that kind of posture all the way. He has no choice but to lean back and take it on the chin. It's not like we're on our way to Cape Town anyway. We'll be home soon.

He has turned this taxi into a tavern, this Hercules, opens a quart every three kilometres and gulps them down like the end of the world is very near. On either flank of the giant man on the seats behind us sits a woman, the one on the right younger and prettier than the one on the left. It surprises me a great deal later, then, that when the watermelon bursts it is the chick on the left the man turns to. He starts a conversation with the woman, their faces so close together they are almost kissing. The woman seems to like the attention. She beams like a little girl. My guess is that this bulky creature, in spite of his godly build, is the same as the majority of us. Beautiful women scare the shit out of him. If I was him I'd have turned to this one on the right, no questions asked.

Some people in this crate might be uncomfortable with it, but I'm perfectly at home with this kind of thing. A grown man boozing, going on and on about nothing while he's at it. His bottles are in a plastic bag between his feet on the floor. Every now and then he bends and winches up one. I grope under my seat with both my feet, trying to touch the stash and knock the bottles over. He won't know who did it. I can't find the stock. My feet are too short. My plan fails. He's starting to irritate me with his blabber, and he's starting to seriously piss everybody off in this khombi. Not that chick next to him though. The man's spatter piles up

147

on her cleavage and she's not bothered. They carry on like rabbits. I turn my focus away from them for a few minutes.

We pass places on our way with names I never knew existed. Leeuwkuil, Keerom, Putfontein, Witpan. The crate rattles on. We don't actually drive past the places themselves but past green boards on either side of the long endlessness that is the road back home, the names on the boards in bold white calligraphy, the directions indicated by way of big white arrows. This world is no chicken coop.

It doesn't take long for the crab to sting. It never does. Now he's plain drunk, and we haven't even made Lichtenburg yet. Bad news for all of us. His volume doubles. I don't think the radio in this taxi can be put up any higher than it is now or the driver would have spun that knob five times to the right a long time ago. I don't think he himself is digging this guy right now. He glowers at him every now and then, in the mirror.

The giant seems to be getting tired, and we're on the verge of the first spell of silence in the transport, when he hears something on the radio that gets him started again. There is some topic going on on the radio about missing children. It is announced by the newsreader in the news that the number of children who went missing the previous festive season had trebled from the year before, the total number of all children under sixteen reported missing having shot up to a staggering thirty-four children. Soon after the presenter makes it a topic and invites the listeners to phone in and share their feelings about the story. As one would expect the phone lines go insane and the masses claim to have lost a lot of faith in the mothers. The jock goes out of his way to remind his callers that fathers also have the same responsibility as far as looking after the child is concerned, does not understand why nobody is starting on them. They won't have it, the man's listeners. As far as they are concerned women, mothers, are the ones to blame when the kids go missing. You only blame the dad when the child goes missing as a result of a snag in the fence, one of them says. I'm not surprised when the stoned halfwit takes over the discussion over and turns it into his one-man show.

'They're right, these people phoning the radio station. Today's mothers are shit. Especially stepmothers. They're the worst, the scum of the land. Dogs. I'm talking from experience.'

We all turn to look at him, and then turn and look away. That seems to be the kind of response he was looking for. It spurs him on, the knowledge that he's got our attention. It pleases him a great deal knowing he's got all of us tuned in to his crap. He goes on and on like a halfwit. And he is a halfwit.

'I bet you my next pay cheque; all the mothers whose children went missing are not the children's real mothers. They're their stepmoms. Yes. Yes. I know it. I've experienced it. I know what I'm talking about. I had the meanest stepmother. Guess who her name was, hmm? Can anybody guess? Boladu. Funny name isn't it? Her heart was full of pus alright. She hated me. She loves me now because I have a job. She doesn't even love me for real. She abused me when I was a kid. Isn't it funny when an old man tells of being abused as a kid? She was a shit mother. Half the things she did to me I will never tell a soul about.'

'Sir, please. We're trying to listen to the radio.'

'Say, lady, do you have stepchildren?'

'That's none of your business.'

'You do. You're somebody's stepmother, aren't you?'

The lady sees no point in arguing with this one. She shuts her trap and looks out the window. Hercules carries on like he was never interrupted.

'I even contemplated running away at some point. I used to cry like a girl, everyday. I had no joy in my life. But I was not going to be a ninny. I knew that at some point I would have to quit being a crybaby and fight back, like a man. It took me a long time to come up with a plan of revenge, just as well because the one I eventually concocted was a stroke of some dead-shit genius. I was going to piss her off, literally. It was a shrewd plan and it worked like a tonic. I started pissing my blankets. That was my way of getting one back on the hag. There was no other way. It needed to be something drastic like that. I was about eleven at the time. They all thought I was sick, that somebody had bewitched me. The crone called an old man into our house who claimed to be a healer. The man whimpered, cried, stomped. He poked fingers into my kidneys and headbutted my bladder, then he assured my stepmom that he'd got rid of the evil. The crone bought the bullshit and paid the clown a chunk of my father's hard-earned money. I took it personal. That was damn plain fucking around. I had to take it up a notch, and I did. I made sure to down two full jugs of water before I turned in that night. It worked. I woke up in a pond the next day, stinking like a horse. I didn't stop. I pissed like a hose, like a broken standpipe. I pissed like a drunk. I pissed like an old man on treatment. She put a potty in my room but I never touched the shit.

She was at sixes and sevens. I drove her insane. She called the shaman again, and the second time around I refused to let the fool touch me. That way there was no chance he was getting a coin of my father's dosh. He couldn't stick around where he was not wanted. He hit the footpath and left me behind with an enraged hag. She chased me around the house, slapped the shits out of me. And that pissed me off even more, so I pissed some more. And my good work started producing results. Only a few weeks at it and the whole house started smelling like a lavatory. I was a happy man. The stink embarrassed the hag like nothing in the world, especially when her friends came to visit. And they never stopped flocking in, her friends who seemed to draw thrills from her misery. I was loving every minute of it. My blankets started growing stains that not the most expensive washing powders could get rid of. I made sure to wake up when the sun was up, everyday, and put them up on the washing line, whistling a tune. The whole thing drove her up the wall, just as I wanted it to. I came back from school one day to find my father sulking like a doll. The crone was gone. He slapped me around a bit, pissed that my incontinence had chased away the love of his life. She was gone for five years, and then she came back. I don't know why she didn't stay away forever.'

The man splutters when he speaks. He's done slagging off his stepmother so he shuts his mouth, for the first time today. He doesn't eject another word until we pass a board with the name Millvale. That is when he shouts for the driver to stop, saying he wants to pee. The driver ignores him and speeds on.

'I can't keep it in anymore, friend. You either pull over or I piss on my seat. Don't be like that, man. I'm asking you

151

nicely. This is not a free ride. I paid money to get on this shit. Do you hear me?'

The driver hits the brakes angrily and pulls over. It's an opportunity to stretch our legs that is grabbed by all of us. We all touch down, the driver included. The women go to one side of the road and the gents to another. The women go a little further down the embankment than the men into the long grass. I look in their direction and my eyes meet an ample couple of brown balloons going down earthwards. I see to it that I stand closest to the loudspeaker when we empty our bladders. In fact, I move in so close our hips are almost touching. He's too pressed and too hammered to give a toss about it and shoo me off. He works his fingers quickly, tears the zip open. A puddle has already collected at our feet before I have even unleashed the first drop. I look at the man's master piece, not stealthily, and the thing is a monster. It spits fire like a cutting torch and gets me feeling sorry for the unlucky tuft of grass. My waist releases my spent liquid and I contribute what little I can to the puddle and I finish before the man. He finishes not too long after me and shakes the asp aggressively. When his hand goes up it nods, when the hand goes down it lifts its head like a cobra warning off an intruder. It spits the last jet of venom into the wind and slithers slowly back into its burrow. We return to our positions in the transport and the impatient driver gets us back on the road again.

Four hours later and a blue taxi with tinted glasses and a reckless driver picks its way out of Rustenburg into Tlhabane, my hood, my homeland, and my heart puffs out with ecstasy. I'm home at last and it ain't no dream. I take ill, struck down by a bout of emotions. My eyes swim like toads in my tears. The khombi reaches my corner and I call it to a stop, eject myself like pus out of a ripe pimple and streak like a creature back to my father's maroon-and-white box. He's in, my old man, and with him is the whole crew. Benedict, Selemo, Ditsebe, Dimpaletse Prince and Malome Jobe – they're all here. It's only Seolo Magang and Maitirelo Malehonyane who are not present. Seolo Magang will surely be at home nursing his bad mouth. I don't know where Maitirelo Malehonyane disappears to every time but I am sure he's gone back there. We're going to miss him. He'll probably only show his face again around here in three years' time. I have never been so happy to see these fellows. I go around shaking all their hands. Malome Jobe says I look like shit, asks me to kiss him and offers me a sip of his drink. I say no thanks to both. I go inside to find my mom watching the box alone. I throw myself into her side and we hug like kittens. She smacks me on the cheek. I love this woman more than anything on this earth. I sit in with her for about an hour or so, but when the urge to hit the streets that has been building up slowly but steadily gives me one solid kick in the groins, I can't stick around for another minute. I tell my mom see you later and hit the avenues to get reunited with this location that I love so much.

Dimpaletse Prince's dwelling is my first stop, and there I run headlong into some crappy news. Dimpaletse Prince's wife is almost flat on her back on the carpet watching the telly with the youngest child, their baby, sitting in a bundle a full two metres off, feeding without a worry in the world on the woman's udder. She tells me that all the other children have returned to Kuruman to stay with their grandma for another year. I don't believe it. I ask her if Lesego has also returned to Kuruman and she tells me yes. My heat fills up with slime. She doesn't even go out of her way to console me. I'm on the verge of bursting into tears and she doesn't even know about it. She just sits there, cold as a pickaxe.

'Will she be coming to visit soon, Mme Aniki?'
'Who?'
'Lesego. Will she at least come and visit when schools close in March?'
'I don't know. I think they'll only show up here again in December. It costs a month's salary and a little bit for all five of them to come up here.'
'The others could always stay behind.'
'Are you crazy? They're my children too.'

I'm getting no joy here. There's no point hanging around. This woman does not understand how hurt I am right now. I step out of her house without saying goodbye and get back out on the streets. I can't believe I survived a week and a half away from this safari park. I see the same busyness, the same faces going up and down of townsmen who I've lived with and among for one hundred years but who I have never known by name. I don't know how I get there but soon I am touching the gate about to push it open and step into Legofi's father's yard. Habit is almighty. Okay, Legofi is a bit of a slowcoach and he flunked his last exams and he will be going back to grade four this year when I continue to grade five and he is still my boy irrespective, but what I am doing here? What if things turn ugly? How could I go and forget and so soon? I can't go inside. I will see the dude again soon, if he's going back to LD and stuff. The front door opens just as I am about to turn and run off. It is the man of the house, he whose shirt was clenched in two fast wrinkles by my dad, pushed around like a nit. I want to run. What if he flays me like he flayed Legofi last year? I'm sure he'd love to get one back on my dad. He calls my name. I stop, frozen like a snowman. He calls me back, invites me to step in and have an early supper with his family. My friend Legofi is in and looking healthy, and quite happy, in spite of what has been going on in his life lately. Mrs Dikutlo is looking silly in a tight shirt, her breasts looking like they will leap out over the low neckline any minute and land on the floor and bounce up and down all over the place like condoms filled with hot water. It seems I'm just on time too, because I have barely touched the chair when the woman of the house sets the table and brings out the chow. She feeds us mutton stew and pap and we tuck in. We eat in silence for a while, until Mr Dikutlo starts asking me about my dad.

'Where's your father, kid?'
  'My dad?'
  'Yes. Where is he?'
  'He's at home.'
  'Okay. Is he well?'
  'Yes. He's fine, Ntate Pagiel.'

He says I must tell my dad he's sorry about what passed between them last year and I nod my head. His wife's stew is really bad. I don't know how an abusive boob like this man tolerates a woman who cooks so badly. I'd send her packing. I take my food very seriously. I get on my feet and say goodbye immediately after burying the last spoon. One of them will probably be left thinking that I'm an underfed glutton who only popped in for the chow. I know it isn't true so I don't really care. I came looking for my boy. They forced that crap down on me. I'm on my way; hope the urge to throw up does not hit me until I'm at least a block away. It's coming, no doubt about that one. No one can

155

keep that kind of muck down. Good thing Legofi doesn't walk me out.

The sun is putting down its chin when I step into my beloved old abode. Malome Jobe and Benedict are at the gate exiting when I come in. I go inside to find my old man at hushed loggerheads with a tall man attired in a checked shirt, a white cap and oversized blue pants. His face is large and oily, and his beard is like Diepeng's pubic hair. His legs, my goodness, his legs are hard as wood and thin as stilts. His shoulders are broad and his breast is larger than two loaves of brown bread put together. His voice is hard as a hammer. He's in my dad's face, spewing threats. My old man winces and shifts and is at pains trying to explain I don't know what. I don't know how to deal with this one. I can't believe those guys closed shop and left my dad alone to fend off this bully. My dad realises that I'm in the room and with a force that he probably didn't dare apply before pulls himself free from the ruffian. I don't think I've ever laid eyes on this guy. My dad is not comfortable with me being in this room right now. He gets rid of me by sending me to Tendai, a colleague of his, to ask him if he's going to work tomorrow. I know it is only to get me out of the way so he and the giant can do their thing in private and I don't give him a hard time. My best guess says the man is a loan shark and that my father owes him a few hundreds. My father confirms an hour later when I come back and ask him. The man is indeed a loan shark. He's actually not a shark anymore, but he used to be one back in the day. My dad tells me he went and borrowed money from the guy some seven and a half years ago. My mother was on a deathbed and she needed an operation. It was an emergency and he did not have a cent in his pockets. He tells me the man's company was more than just a cash loan thing but had other things going on the side, illegal things. My dad knew nothing of the stuff going on on the side of course. All he wanted was a loan, and he got it. He says the man's company was closed down soon after he got the loan after a police raid that uncovered many horrors. The coppers took him down and took him in, and my dad couldn't honour the contract and make any repayments because the place was shut down. The man is back now, almost eight years later. He's looking for his dosh and he's not taking crap. My dad says they reached an agreement earlier, he and the loan shark, that he will pay him back everything he owes him over the next four months. In the meantime, though, he's taken our TV as security. My dad sits worrying in the one-sitter. I tell him after a while that Tendai says he hasn't decided yet and he has no idea what I'm talking about. He points at the empty TV stand and promises he'll sort it out tomorrow.

'It's okay, Dad. Don't worry about it too much.'
    'It's not okay, Prof. You loved that TV.'

I'm not at home when he comes back from work the next day. When I get home I find there's a brand new picture machine on the stand, only a smaller one.

We're going back to school tomorrow. What a long break it's been. I wonder if I can even still spell my name. My dad does not sit in the one-sitter sulking tonight but he's outside with his mates doing what they do every night. My mom calls me to their bedroom to have me fit my new school uniform for the second time since it was bought last year. I have lost quite some weight this past week or so and my skinny neck sticks out my new shirt's firm collar like a very sore thumb. The uniform looks okay in spite of the thin neck sticking out so I get out of it and go to bed. I can't have bloodshot eyes on my very first day back from such a long break. Wonder if I will make new friends this year. Wonder if I'll start chasing after girls.

I am in my room and the light is off. My mom has washed my bedclothes and my blankets smell like flowers. I'm not asleep yet. The door opens and shuts and the plastic chair next to my desk that I sit on when I study is drawn. It's my dad. The smell of his food infiltrates my blankets. He's hiding from his buddies. He shares a lot with those guys, but never his food. I don't know why he chose my room tonight though. He always goes and wolfs in his and Mom's bedroom. I'm not thrilled. This smell will be hanging in here until the morning. The spoon assaults the plate non-stop and I know he will be back outside with the pack soon, and they won't know what he's been getting up to. I'm still listening to his jaws chomping on the chow when he extends a warm hand and touches my bare foot that sticks out from the covers like a horn. My anger evaporates. He probably thinks I'm asleep, but I'm not. Warm feelings spread through my system. Tears soak through my pillow. I wonder if he's got tears in his eyes too. Our moment is interrupted by a holler from outside.

'Rastaman. Hey, Rasta. Come on out, man, what are you doing in there? We're getting lonely on our own out here, friend.'

He responds with a low grumble, mouth full to the palate with half-chewed food.

'Half-witted wretches. Will they bloody die if they don't know where I am for two minutes?'

He plonks the plate on my study desk and shuffles out cussing. I pull my foot back in the covers and drop off like a zombie.

JLF JACANA LITERARY FOUNDATION

Other Jacana Literary Foundation Titles

African Delights
Siphiwo Mahala

Hear Me Alone
Thando Mgqolozana

*The Zombie
and the Moon*
Peter Merrington